"Convince Me That This Marriage Is What You Really Want, Susannah."

His gaze dropped to her lips. The taste of his kiss slid through her veins. This was what she'd expected last night and she'd armed herself against the assault. Now he'd caught her unprepared. She needed to breathe, to ease the swell of emotion in her chest. "I can't stay, Donovan."

"I'm afraid you have no choice."

"How long are you holding me hostage?" she asked.

"As long as it takes," he said, then stepped closer.

Dear Reader,

If you've read my PRINCES OF THE OUTBACK trilogy then you may remember Susannah Horton. Although she didn't appear on the page, Susannah played a vital, indispensable role as Alex Carlisle's intended bride. In *The Ruthless Groom,* she was the catalyst that brought Alex and Zara together…and one of the obstacles that kept them apart.

The possibility of creating a happily-ever-after for Susannah only struck after I'd finished writing *The Ruthless Groom,* and during the final edits I hurriedly added some hints of her future story. At that stage I had no idea what her story would be, only that she'd run away from her wedding because of "a mystery man." That man would have to be very special, I knew, and her reason for running high-stakes. And that was all I knew.

To those readers who've been eagerly awaiting Susannah's story—here it is! I hope you enjoy her journey from a conveniently arranged engagement to a marriage based purely—and inconveniently—on love. I also hope you enjoy your reading journey to Tasmania, Australia's southernmost island state. Stranger's Bay and Charlotte Island are both fictitious but, I hope, reflective of the wild natural beauty and dramatic scenery for which Tasmania is known.

Cheers from the Land Down Under,

Bronwyn Jameson

BRONWYN JAMESON

TYCOON'S ONE-NIGHT REVENGE

Silhouette
Desire

Published by Silhouette Books
America's Publisher of Contemporary Romance

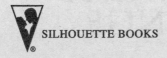

SILHOUETTE BOOKS

ISBN-13: 978-0-373-76865-3
ISBN-10:   0-373-76865-6

TYCOON'S ONE-NIGHT REVENGE

BRONWYN JAMESON

Bronwyn Jameson spent most of her childhood with her head buried in a book. It seemed only fitting that she turn her love of romance fiction into a career, creating the kind of stories she's always loved to read. Her books have won many accolades including an Emma Darcy Award, an Aspen Gold, a Write Touch Readers Award, an Anne Bonney Readers' Choice, and in 2006 she was a triple RITA® Award finalist and nominated as *Romantic Times BOOKreviews* Series Storyteller of the Year.

Bronwyn shares an idyllic piece of the Australian farming heartland with her husband, three sons, three dogs, a few thousand sheep, several horses and the occasional wallaby or echidna. She still spends most of her time with her head stuck in a book, sometimes writing, sometimes reading and always avoiding housework.

You can contact Bronwyn via her Web site at www.bronwynjameson.com.

With heartfelt thanks to the mates who talked,
and at times walked, me through this story
in one or more of its many incarnations.
Trish, Yvonne, Emilie, Fiona, Anne: you guys rock!

One

So, she'd come. Sooner than Donovan Keane had anticipated, given the weather and the travel necessary to reach the resort's remote location. And, Van noted with satisfaction, she'd come alone.

Good.

A grim half smile tugged at the corners of his mouth as he watched her dismiss the bellhop's substantial umbrella and jog up the steps toward reception. Under the shelter of the portico she paused to acknowledge the doorman, and something in the swing of her red-gold hair and the lift of her hand triggered a weird flash of déjà vu. For a fraction of a second, time vacillated from present to past, between dream and reality.

Then she disappeared inside the building, gone in a

flurry of long legs and designer raincoat, leaving Van alone and stripped of his satisfied smile.

Punching gloved fist against palm, he searched his memory but came up blank. "Big surprise," he told a captive audience of weight stations and treadmills.

He'd identified Susannah Horton the second he caught sight of her arrival through the rain-streaked window. But that recognition was due to the number of photos he'd viewed during the past weeks of intensive research—Australian society cameras loved the local hotel heiress—and not from the weekend she'd spent in his company. Shoving away from the window, Van shook the tight grip of frustration from his muscles and circled the punching bag he'd deserted minutes earlier.

He'd flown in from San Francisco the previous morning, but twenty-four hours at The Palisades at Stranger's Bay, the Tasmanian resort where they'd supposedly spent that weekend, had done nothing to fill the dark hole in his memory. Hell, he'd come within a whisker of buying the place, yet nothing rang any bells. Not his flight into Australia's island state, not the helicopter transfer to the isolated retreat. Not even his first stunning view of the scattered villas perched high on a rocky promontory overlooking the southern ocean.

Nothing. *Thud.* Nada. *Thud.* Zilch. *Thud.*

Van hit the punching bag with a lethal barrage of punches that did little to soothe his frustration. The insistent internal burn came from more than the forgotten weekend, more than losing the prime property to an Australian hotel group. It stemmed from *how* he'd lost out.

The below-the-belt punch had been thrown while he

lay unconscious in an ICU, incapable of defending himself let alone fighting back. *Thud.* A knockout counterbid, perfectly timed and perfectly presented. *Thud.* And all due to a treacherous redhead named Susannah Horton. *Thudthudthud.*

Despite the veiled threat in the voice mail he'd left last night, he hadn't expected her to turn up so promptly. At best, he'd expected a return call. At worst, another don't-you-dare-call-again reply from her mother. The fact that Susannah had scurried down here without any advance warning or any entourage in tow, suggested he hadn't misread the signs.

She'd come because he'd hit a vein, and she hadn't wasted a minute seeking him out here in the resort's state-of-the-art fitness centre.

He hadn't heard her entrance, but he caught a glimpse of reflected movement in the expansive window. And a jolt of awareness travelled the length of his spine, strong enough that his next punch miscued and slid off the side of the bag. Recovering, he delivered a final combination of punches, sharp, swift, relentless, until his breath rasped in his lungs and his inner physical therapist barked, *enough!*

Then he dispensed with the boxing gloves and pulled on a T-shirt. Snagging his towel and water bottle he turned, and, dodging the arc of the still swinging bag, started toward the plush reception area. As he walked, he drank from his bottle and he drank in the woman.

Up close Susannah Horton packed even more punch than that first glimpse through glass and rain. She wasn't a bombshell; her beauty was more about class than

flash. Tall, willowy, feminine. Generous lips balanced
by a long, straight nose. Red-gold hair and the kind of
redhead's complexion that would burn in the sun. Green
eyes that tilted upward and smoked with wariness.

Until that second, he'd harboured a lingering doubt
over how they'd spent their days, and nights, that July
weekend. He couldn't recall one damn detail. All he had
to go on was Miriam Horton's word—and hadn't that
been one helluva phone conversation!—and his own
instincts. Those he trusted. And when his eyes locked
on hers, when he detected the suppressed heat in their
sea-green depths, his body responded with a powerful
jolt of elemental recognition. As he came to a halt in
front of her, his instincts hummed like a mesotron.

Oh, yeah, she'd slept with him, all right.

And then she'd really screwed him over.

Susannah thought she was ready for this moment.
Since hearing his voice mail last night, she'd had
enough time to prepare. More than once she'd cursed
herself for her impulsive, panicky reaction to his voice
mail. More than once she'd considered turning straight
around and flying back home.

But what good would that have done? She hadn't
imagined the aggressive edge to that recorded message
any more than she'd misheard the threat inherent in
his words. She may not have adopted her usual ana-
lytical approach before deciding to fly down here—
impulsiveness seemed to be a feature of her dealings
with Donovan Keane—but she had made the right
decision.

And after five hours of travelling and analysing, Susannah's initial anxiety had developed a decent head of indignation. After weeks of ignoring her calls, he'd turned up, two months later, making threats that sounded ominously close to blackmail. She had many, many regrets about that weekend and its aftermath, but she was not the guilty party. And the more she thought about his message, the more questions it raised.

In that frame of mind she'd marched into The Palisades' gym and found Donovan naked from his low-slung sweatpants up, muscles rippling with lean strength as he pummelled that unfortunate hunk of leather into submission. All the simmering indignation had deserted her mind. She was left empty, hollow, underprepared, and so *so* susceptible to the flood of sensations that came from seeing him again.

When he turned and his eyes locked on hers, the blow to her senses was more powerful than any he'd thrown against the leather bag.

It was just like the first time they'd met, the first time she became the sole focus of that riveting silver-grey gaze. She experienced the same rush of awareness, the same slow somersault in her stomach, the same sweet explosion of warmth in her skin.

Instantly entranced. At a loss. Slow to react.

So slow that he'd come to a halt in front of her before she realised what was wrong with this picture. It was too much like that first meeting. The way he was silently taking her all in, not like a lover, not even like an acquaintance, but almost like a stranger.

What was going on? Did he not remember her? Was

this even the same man she'd fallen for with such uncharacteristic haste on that wintry July weekend?

"Donovan?" she asked in a second's uncertainty.

"Were you expecting someone else?"

Head tilted at a slight angle, he narrowed his eyes in
an expression as familiar as the defined angle of his
cheekbones and the fullness of his bottom lip. Oh, yes,
this was Donovan Keane. His hair cut ruthlessly short,
his face sharper and harder, his expression as cold as an
Antarctic wind, but definitely Donovan.

"After the tone of your message, I wasn't sure what to
expect," she replied, battling to collect her scrambled composure. "Although I must say I didn't expect you to look
me over as if you were having trouble remembering me."

He'd lifted the towel slung around his neck to wipe the
sheen of perspiration from his face, but that didn't disguise
the flicker of emotion deep in his eyes. Not belated friend-
liness. Not the teasing humour that had caught her off
guard so many times the weekend they'd met.

"My message wasn't clear?" he asked.

"Frankly, no, it wasn't."

The towel paused midswipe and in the hard set of his
jaw and the thin line of his lips, Susannah recognised
the signs of restraint. He wasn't cold and distant; he was
struggling to hide his anger. "What part do I need to
make clearer?"

Bewildered by his hostility, she shook her head. "The
part where you're so angry with me."

"You can drop the innocent act, Goldilocks. You
know what this is about."

Innocent act? Goldilocks?

Susannah's confusion sharpened with irritation. "I can assure you, this is no act."

"Then let me spell it out for you. Right after our weekend together—a weekend you spent in my well-paid employment—my bid to acquire this resort was rejected."

"Your bid was bettered."

"By Carlisle Hotel Group, which is headed by your close friend and business ally, Alex Carlisle."

Was he implying that things weren't aboveboard? "Alex's bid was legitimate."

"So I was led to believe. Imagine my surprise when I discovered, a week ago, that he's also your fiancé. Tell me," he continued conversationally, "did he suggest you sweet-talk me into revealing details of my proposal? Was that how he perfected a counterbid so quickly?"

"That makes no sense," she fired back, her composure splintered by that outrageous accusation. "Your recollection of that weekend appears to be seriously flawed."

A muscle in his cheek jumped but he replied in the same deceptively even tone. "Perhaps you had better refresh my memory."

"*You* hired *me*. You had to sweet-talk me into changing my schedule to take the job. I warned you there could be a conflict of interest with my mother owning a significant stake in The Palisades, but you insisted. You wanted me."

For a long moment, their gazes clashed. The air between them crackled with animosity and with a different kind of heat, the kind that flared from those last three words. *You wanted me.* And he had—there'd been no disputing the physicality of his desire—but it had been secondary to the real reason he'd sought the services of her private-concierge business.

"You wanted me," she said tightly, "because of my mother's shareholding. You wanted my recommendation in her ear to ensure all the board voted yes to your proposal. But once you'd had me, you got complacent. You only had to play nice a little longer and your bid would have won approval."

His eyes narrowed. "I didn't play nice?"

"When you went back to America, you shouldn't have screened my calls. I wasn't about to make a pest of myself. All you had to say was 'We had fun, Susannah, but we're not looking for the same thing here. Let's leave it at that.' If you hadn't thought your bid was in the bag...if you'd taken my calls instead of hiding behind your assistant—"

She broke off, annoyed at revealing how much she'd let that stonewalling silence hurt. For letting the emotion seep into her words and to rasp the edges of her voice. But she straightened her shoulders and met the stillness of his gaze with quiet dignity. "All you had to do was pick up the phone, Donovan. Just once."

For a short beat his eyes remained on hers, their depths stark with what looked like frustration, and Susannah braced herself for his next attack. But he only shook his head briefly before turning to pace the short distance to the window. Hands on hips, he stared out into the sodden landscape and belatedly she realised that the rain had relented to a thin drizzle, painting the glass a misty grey.

The same colour as his morning eyes, she recalled with a jab of regret, and when he swung around, those eyes fixed on hers without a hint of that remembered softness. "Let me get this straight. You're saying I lost an eight-figure deal I'd spent months pursuing because I didn't return your calls?"

Put like that it sounded like a game of school-yard pettiness, and when Donovan exhaled a disbelieving huff of breath, Susannah knew he was thinking the same. The awful truth churned sickly in her stomach. He was right. There had been an element of "the hell with you" in her decision, but there'd been a whole lot more going on, as well.

Lifting her chin, she met his gaze across the blue-matted floor. "It was more complicated than that."

"The complication being Alex Carlisle. Your fiancé."

"That was one thing," she replied carefully. One thing that Donovan Keane should not have known.

"And it brings us to my original question."

With the same slow, deliberate pace as he imbued the words, he started back toward her and the new determination in his expression caused a shiver of disquiet in Susannah's skin. When he stopped right in front of her, her heartbeat skittered with anxiety. She didn't have to ask which question. She knew he referred to the one he'd left on her voice mail last night.

Does your fiancé know you slept with me?

The unspoken question arced between them for several seconds in the tense stillness. Susannah didn't have to say a word. She knew he'd read the answer in her eyes and that any denial wouldn't be worth the breath it took, yet one thing needed saying. One very important thing.

"I wasn't engaged to Alex then."

"Yet you hared down here today. I can only assume you want to protect your dirty little secret."

Susannah's eyes widened with the sting of those words. They cheapened what she'd once thought special, but then she'd been a prize fool to think they'd shared anything other than a one-weekend stand. "Since you haven't contacted Alex, I can only assume you want something from me in return for keeping quiet about my...error in judgment?"

Something flared in his eyes, a brief indication that he'd noticed her choice of words. *Score one, Susannah.* Her battered ego rallied instantly.

"Why did you come back here, Donovan?" she asked. "What do you want from me?"

"I want to know how and when Carlisle became involved in this deal. The Palisades wasn't officially on the market, I did all the legwork, I convinced them to sell." His gaze locked on hers, gimlet sharp and merciless. "Did you take the deal to him?"

"Yes," Susannah admitted after a moment. "But only—"

"No buts or onlys. You brought him into this deal, you can take him out again."

"How do you expect me to do that?" Her voice rose, incredulous. "Horton's management accepted the Carlisle offer. The contracts are drawn."

"Drawn, but not signed."

Of course the contracts weren't signed—they wouldn't be until both sides of the deal she'd negotiated with Alex were fulfilled.

"As for how—" he paused to pull on a sweatshirt "—I don't care. That's your problem."

Stunned by the audacity of his demand, Susannah took several seconds to realise what the sweatshirt meant. By then he'd gathered towel and water. "You're leaving?" she asked on a note of alarm.

"We've said all that needs to be said for now. I'll leave you to make your phone calls."

Every instinct screamed at her to stop him, to explain the impossibility of what he asked, but as much as she railed against admitting it, he was right. She needed to think, to chart her options, to decide who to call.

Her mind had started to chew over that conundrum when he paused at the door.

"One of those calls should be to your mother," he said, as if he'd read her mind. "Ask her what she knows about me returning your calls. And while you're chatting, you might want to get your stories straight about your engagement."

He *had* called.

A week ago, according to Miriam Horton, who'd taken the call at the Melbourne office of Susannah's concierge service. Her mother wasn't a permanent employee, God forbid, but she helped out when necessary. Sometimes the need wasn't Susannah's, but more often Miriam's. Despite her many charity committees and her directorship at Horton Holdings, Miriam still needed more to fill the chasm created by her husband's death three years ago.

She needed to be needed, a condition Susannah understood all too well.

What Susannah didn't understand was Miriam's failure to pass on the news of Donovan's call. *A week ago.* A week of days spent working alongside her mother every day, preparing her for Susannah's absence over the next two weeks.

In the manager's office of The Palisades, Susannah released her icy clutch on the phone and paced to the window. How could her mother have kept this to herself?

"You were about to leave with Alex, to visit the Carlisle family's ranch," she had justified. "I know how uptight you were about meeting his mother and convincing his brothers he'd made the right choice of wife. On top of your business stress, I didn't want to load you with another burden."

"A client is never a burden," Susannah had reminded her.

"A client?" Miriam tsked her disapproval. "We both know Donovan Keane transcended that boundary."

Susannah ignored the jibe and concentrated on the question at hand. "You should have told me he called."

"What good would that have done, darling?"

I would have been warned of his imminent reappearance, I could have prepared my explanation, I might not have made an ill-informed goose of myself. "I would not have been caught out when he called back."

There'd been a moment's pause, the sound of air being drawn through delicate nostrils. "I told him, in no uncertain terms, never to call you again."

"That was not your place."

"It is always a mother's place to protect her child," Miriam countered, "as you will discover once you are a mother. That man used you, darling, and then he cast you aside. Now you're engaged to marry an honourable man whose word you can trust. Surely I don't need to remind you of that?"

Of course she didn't, but Donovan's final sling about getting the facts straight rang in her ears. "What, exactly, did you tell him about my engagement?"

"I don't recall my exact words."

"Did you mention when I accepted Alex's proposal?" When her mother *hmmed* vaguely, Susannah went very still. Miriam Horton did not do vague. Her sharp-as-a-whip recall of names, places, facts was legendary in Melbourne society circles. It also made her a valuable, if aggravating, member of Susannah's *At Your Service* team. "Did you tell him I was engaged when we met? When we came down here for that weekend?"

"He may have gleaned that impression, but I don't see why that should be an issue."

Caught between exasperation and a sinking sense of acceptance, Susannah pinched the bridge of her nose. At least now she understood why he'd looked at her so differently, why he'd been so scathing, why he'd sensed collusion between her and Alex.

"You said he called," Miriam continued.

"Last night. He's here, Mother. In Australia."

"Please tell me you're not seeing him, Susannah. Please tell me this isn't why Alex called, asking if I knew where you'd gone today. He sounded very unlike himself, edgy and short and slightly…annoyed."

More than slightly, Susannah predicted, turning away from the window with a heavy sigh. And she didn't blame him. After deciding to fly down here in the early hours of this morning, she'd tried to call him, to tell him she was going away to think things over, but he hadn't answered his phone...and wasn't *that* becoming the story of her life?

In her frantic rush to organize travel and get to the airport in time for her flight, she'd left the task of contacting him to her half sister. Zara would have delivered the message, Susannah had no doubt. She also wouldn't have been daunted by Alex or bullied into revealing anything more than the message.

However, Susannah had learned in the last thirty minutes how easily the message-delivery system could go pear-shaped...and the consequences of miscommunication. The idea of dealing with another thwarted alpha-on-a-mission filled her with trepidation, but she had to call Alex. She had to let him know she was all right, that she hadn't walked out on him, that she'd simply panicked when faced with a tricky problem from her past. She still intended to marry him just as soon as they could schedule a time and a celebrant.

In several decisive strides, she crossed to the desk and picked up the landline phone. There was no cell coverage in this remote corner of the country, which was a plus or a minus for the resort depending on the client. She imagined both Alex and Zara would have tried to contact her, that they would both be puzzled by her uncharacteristic "disappearance," since she'd left no clue as to her destination and never went anywhere without her phone.

With all the misunderstandings swirling in the air,

protecting her location had turned out to be a smart move. A face-off between Donovan and Alex could only end in an ugly confrontation. She had created this twisted mess and she needed to unravel it.

Starting with a phone call to Alex, and finishing with the explanation Donovan deserved.

Two

From a sheltered perch in his villa's hot tub, Van tracked the bobbing progress of the yellow umbrella as it dipped in and out of sight behind clusters of brush and jutting outcrops of rock. As well as sealed roadways that provided vehicular access to the accommodations, a series of rustic walking paths traversed the steeply sloped headland…although he didn't think Susannah was taking a nice, invigorating stroll in the rain.

Van had tried that himself after leaving the fitness centre—more at a run than a walk—before easing his overworked muscles into the swirling water. To help him relax, a bottle of pinot noir sat open at his side. The combination had been working a treat until he spotted the zigzagging umbrella zeroing in on his ridgetop location.

It had been ninety minutes since they spoke. Ninety

minutes to make her phone calls, to compare notes, to concoct whatever comeback she brought back to the table. And that's what she would do. Van had no illusions about that. If her stake in this deal wasn't high, she would not have hared down here today. She wouldn't have reacted so strongly to his accusations. She would have shrugged them off or called his bluff by handing him Alex Carlisle's business card.

Earlier he'd been tense and on guard, wary of giving away his one point of weakness. If she'd latched on to his deficient memory of that weekend, she could have grabbed a huge advantage. Instead she'd handed him the gift of her knowledge and the desire to unwrap it. If he asked the right questions or made suitable leading statements, she would fill in some of the memory gaps…and after meeting her, he wanted more than ever to fill in those gaps.

It wasn't only her beauty—expected, given the pictures he'd seen—but her attitude. He didn't recall if she'd used the phrase *how dare you accuse me*, but that was the message trumpeted by her defensive stance and haughty gaze.

Who would have thought that affronted dignity could be so damn arousing? Or that wintergreen eyes could light a flame in his blood?

Despite the miles he'd run through the rain, despite the blast of icy wind against his exposed skin, the heat of their encounter still licked through his body. It was no surprise that she'd lured him into her bed on that forgotten weekend. Or, if he wanted to believe her version of events, how much he'd have enjoyed doing the luring. He could imagine how easily the seduction would have gone down.

Hello, I'm Susannah, a few seconds tangling in those deceptively cool eyes, and she could have led him away…or pushed him down to the floor and taken him there.

The fact that he didn't remember any of the *wheres* or *whens* or *how many times* kicked through him, but not with the same impact as before. Now the frustration was tempered by satisfaction with how their first meeting had played out, as well as anticipation for their upcoming encounter.

He'd done the hard work, now he intended treating himself to a little entertainment.

When she disappeared behind the casuarinas that screened the approach to his villa, he planted both hands on the timber deck and hauled himself out of the water. For an evil beat of time, he contemplated walking to the door as he was. Naked, wet and, now he'd started thinking about who he'd be greeting at the door, aroused.

But he wrapped himself in one of the resort-issue robes, not through any sense of modesty, but for the same reason he'd donned a shirt before facing her in the gym. He didn't want her eyes drawn to the scars or her mind to their cause. He preferred to keep that in reserve, to play only if absolutely necessary.

With the bottle and emptied glass swinging from one hand, he headed for the sliders that separated terrace from living area. Despite the shelter afforded by the surrounding garden, a wet southeasterly gusted in and plastered the towelling to his damp thighs. It was the kind of unruly blast that could turn a woman's umbrella inside out, but when he opened the door, Susannah Horton stood on his doorstep, looking disappointingly dry in her tightly buttoned and belted raincoat.

She also wore a look of determined poise, although that faltered slightly when she took in his state of dress. It was the barest glance, before her eyes fixed resolutely on his face, but the trace of heat in her cheeks and eyes gave away her discomfiture. "I'm sorry," she said quickly. "I've caught you in the shower."

"The hot tub, actually. Would you care to join me?"

She blinked once in surprise before recovering swiftly. "Thank you, but I'll take a rain check."

Beautiful, poised *and* a sense of irony. Van's appreciation of Susannah Horton grew by the second. "The tub's sheltered, the water's warm, the wine's open." He saluted her with his glass. "I highly recommend it."

"I didn't bring my swimsuit."

"Nor did I," Van said evenly. "I don't see that as a problem."

The colour in her cheeks sharpened, but she held his gaze steadily. "Nor would I, but we've done all the tubbing we will ever do together."

"I gather it's my company you object to, and yet here you are."

"Briefly. I'm leaving at four."

"Do you always schedule your time this precisely?"

"Only when I have a flight to catch," she replied smartly, and Van realised she was talking about leaving the resort rather than his villa. All day, the weather had been iffy for the necessary helicopter transfer. He wouldn't bet on anyone going anywhere until after this storm front passed, but he figured she would find that out for herself soon enough.

Opening the door wider, he waved his wineglass toward the cosy interior. "I'm disappointed you're passing on the tub, but there's still the wine. Why don't you come in and I'll get you a glass?"

Her elegantly shod feet remained rooted to the spot and, by the look on her face, he might as well have invited her into the wolves' den. He managed to refrain from baring his teeth. "You might be all snug in your buttoned-up coat, but I'm freezing my ass…ets off here."

"Perhaps you should put some clothes on," she suggested. Taking obvious care to avoid contact with anything close to his assets, she edged through the doorway.

No, Van decided with a perverse little smile as he closed the door. *I prefer the robe, just to keep you on edge.*

And just to keep himself on edge he watched her walk away in skinny-heeled boots that were designed to highlight the sexy arch of her calves and the sway of her hips. "Why don't you take your coat off," he said, following her through to the living room. "Make yourself at home. I'll pour your—"

"This isn't a social visit," she replied crisply, still walking, circling the room as if she couldn't decide where to plant her sexy heels. "No wine for me."

"So it's business." Van deposited glass and bottle on the table. "I'm impressed. I didn't think you'd have managed to talk Carlisle around in such a short time."

That brought her up short in front of a leather sofa. She didn't sit. Shoulders straight and chin high, she turned to face him. "I haven't spoken to Alex yet. I may not be able to reach him until Monday."

Van settled his hips against the edge of the dining table and crossed his arms across his chest. Playtime was over…for now. "You can't reach your fiancé on weekends?"

"He isn't answering any of his phones, which means he is not in his office or at his home. I will continue to try his cell, but if he's out of the coverage area—" she shrugged "—there's nothing else I can do."

"Convenient."

"Not particularly," she countered without missing a beat, although her gaze sharpened as his barb found its mark. "I would prefer if I could reach him."

"How about your mother? Is she answering any of her phones?"

"Yes, I have spoken with her and she told me about your call last weekend. I'm sorry that she didn't tell me about that and I'm even more sorry that she mislead you about my engagement."

Van studied her closely for a second. Playtime was definitely over. "Are you telling me you're not engaged to Alex Carlisle?"

"I wasn't in July. I am now." Her gaze narrowed on his. "Why do I get the feeling that you don't believe me?"

"Because, apart from your mother, I haven't managed to find anyone who knows about it. Scores of mentions of you and Carlisle in business and society columns, yet no mention of pending nuptials."

"Which is exactly the way we like it," she said with bite. Then, as if annoyed with that minishow of temper, she pressed her lips together and composed herself before continuing in a more measured tone. "Both our families are high profile, especially the Carlisles, and we don't want a media circus surrounding our wedding plans. Alex decided—we both decided," she amended quickly, "not to make an announcement until after we're married."

"And when will that be?"

For the first time, her eyes shifted nervously and she lifted a hand—her left hand—in a vague fluttery gesture. "I...we haven't settled on a definite date."

Van's eyes shifted to her hand and a grim punch of satisfaction drove him to his feet. "Soon?"

"Yes," she said, her uneasy gaze steadying and settling. "Very soon."

Ever since he'd opened the door, Susannah had been at a distinct disadvantage. Everything from the carelessly knotted robe, to the teasing glint in his eyes, to the suggestion they get naked together in the hot tub, rang with unwanted memories. Inside the villa it was even worse. How could she concentrate when every place they'd kissed, touched and ended up naked was right in front of her eyes?

Of course she'd forced herself to keep those eyes stoically trained on his face, and the tricky nuances of their dialogue had managed to push everything—including his lack of clothes—to the fringes of her mind.

Until now.

As he moved closer, the edges of her vision and the core of her senses swam with the knowledge of how little he wore and how exposed she felt. Her heartbeat thickened and bumped painfully hard against her ribs. She didn't know what he wanted, why he'd suddenly shoved to his feet, why that narrowed gaze had suddenly focussed so intently on her—

"Why aren't you wearing a ring?"

Susannah stared back at him. She opened her mouth, found no answer and shut it again. In that beat of time, he picked up her left hand.

"Isn't that the usual procedure when you're engaged to be married? A diamond ring on this finger?"

He illustrated by grazing her ring finger with the pad of his thumb. It was a simple touch, but he stood close enough that she breathed the male heat of his skin, and her body acknowledged a myriad of other touches that were not so innocent. Warmth suffused her skin and pooled low in her belly but she fought it gamely. "I don't have an engagement ring."

"Carlisle didn't buy you a diamond? What did he give you then? A share package? Expansion capital? An exclusive agreement to use your service in the Carlisle hotel chain?"

His voice was soft and mocking, but his watchful eyes never left hers. Wasn't this why she'd hiked up here—to dispel the misconceptions and tell him the truth? To explain why the demand he'd made of her was impossible to deliver? Her stomach churned with trepidation, but she had to try.

"He offered a rescue package for my business."

"You're in financial trouble?"

Susannah tugged her hand free, but the warmth of that contact still tingled through her skin along with the shame of admitting her sorry business plight. Both flustered her; she could feel the heat in her face and couldn't stop it leaking into her voice. "I expanded too fast, my ideas were too grand and I wanted to prove I was capable of succeeding on my own. I made a poor borrowing choice and, yes, I've struggled with the debt."

"I'm finding that hard to fathom. You're a Horton. Your parents—"

"I didn't want their help," she cut in. "I didn't want to use my father's money. That was the point. You know why." She'd told him about her father's secret life and why she'd left the family company to start her own business, but there was something in his expression that suggested she should add this to the list of things he'd forgotten from their weekend.

"Accepting your parents' help is different to accepting help from your husband-to-be?" he asked.

"Yes," she said fiercely, "it absolutely is. This is not a one-sided situation."

"What *does* Carlisle get in return for his investment?"

"He gets me."

Their gazes clashed for a long, heated moment. Something flickered in Donovan's eyes, a hint of anger or denial that was quickly doused. He drew back and studied her with undisguised disapproval. "So, he's buying himself a wife. A blue-blooded Horton with all the right credentials and a resort on the side."

That mocking arrow found its target but Susannah didn't flinch. She held no illusions about the marriage contract she'd entered into. She understood the terms; she'd spent a full week dissecting them before reaching her decision. Lifting her chin, she met her adversary's disparaging gaze. "Alex believes he's getting a bargain."

"But then he doesn't know everything about you, does he?"

"I don't know what you're talking about."

"You do," he countered, his voice a silky contrast to the steel of his gaze. "What does your Alex think about his wife sleeping with clients?"

"His *wife* may have made some poor choices in the past, but that was before she made any vows of fidelity. Once she committed to one man, she would never cheat. She knows the hurt that can inflict on everyone involved."

"Have you made many of these poor choices?"

"Just one comes to mind."

"It can't have been all bad," he said, and their gazes tangled for an unnervingly quiet second. She couldn't lie, she couldn't construct a smart retort. She doubted she could even hide the truth that ached in her chest from showing in her eyes.

Memories, she told herself. *It is nothing but false memories.*

"No," she managed finally. "Not all bad. I learned a valuable lesson about making rash choices, about staying true to my naturally cautious nature. About thinking my actions through to the consequences. I learned to ask, why does this man want me? And to be honest with the answers."

Heat flared in his quicksilver eyes. "You don't believe I could have just wanted you?"

"You wanted me," she replied, "and you made sure

you got me. You just didn't disclose your reasons until after you'd had me."

A muscle ticked in his cheek and his mouth tightened in an uncompromising line, but for a fraction of a second, she imagined a softened note of regret in his eyes. Then he turned and started toward the kitchen. He'd only taken a half-dozen strides—she'd barely had time to suck in a deep breath to ease the pounding in her chest—when he swung back around to face her.

Oh, yes, she'd definitely imagined the softening. Now his expression was inscrutable, but the sharp lines of his cheekbones and the straight set of his mouth lent him a hard, dangerous aura. Her instincts shivered back to high alert.

"You didn't mention this place." He indicated his surroundings with a sweep of his hand. "Where does it fit into the Carlisle-Horton merger?"

"It didn't initially, not until after Alex proposed."

"Which was when?"

Susannah pressed her lips together and withheld her none-of-your-business response. He wanted the facts; she would give him the facts. Then, perhaps, he might see the impossibility of his quest. "In late July, just after our weekend. I was feeling a little…burned by that experience."

"And so you were receptive to a cold, business-contract proposal?"

"I was receptive to his honesty," she replied, and was rewarded by the glint of irritation in his eyes. Good. He'd delivered enough backhanded blows, he deserved to take one back. "I weighed up the pros and cons. I talked it over with my mother, and in the process, she found out what had happened between us. To say she wasn't happy would be an understatement."

"Your mother requires approval of your lovers?"

"She wasn't happy that you'd used me to influence your bid. She withdrew her approval."

The spark of irritation she'd lit in his eyes turned cold and hard. "She occupies one seat in that boardroom. Are you saying the rest of the board agreed?"

"Not immediately but as Edward Horton's widow her opinion holds some sway. She argued against your business scruples and they listened but they also had your bid on the table. So my mother asked for a week to come up with an alternate buyer."

"So she found Carlisle and added a clause to the marriage contract. 'You can have my daughter, but only if you better the bid we have for The Palisades.'" He made a short, rough sound, the perfect punctuation for the scathing tone of his delivery. "And that's where you came in, with your intimate knowledge of my bid."

"No," Susannah objected vehemently. "I had no part in that."

"Are you saying this was all concocted between your mother and Carlisle? Without your knowledge?"

"I agreed to the marriage contract. I agreed to all the terms, including The Palisades. I didn't want you to get this place. I didn't want to ever see you again." An objection lit his eyes and she hurried on, not wanting to argue that point. "But I did not divulge anything about your bid. How could I have known what to divulge, for heaven's sake? Do you think I read your mind or that you murmured sweet multimillion-dollar figures in your sleep or that I sneaked a look at your files?"

Susannah stopped, her eyes widening at the stillness in his face. He *did* think that. She shook her head slowly and coughed out a disbelieving laugh.

"How, exactly, do you think I might have managed that? We spent all our time here—" she waved her arm, indicating the rooms around them, but her tone was as cool and disparaging as the subject demanded "—in the villa I had booked. Do you think that after wearing you out in the bedroom, I picked your room key from your pocket and clambered down the cliffside in the dead of night to peek at your laptop?"

Consternation tightened the line of his brows, but Susannah was beyond dissecting what he was thinking or feeling or pretending not to feel. Always she had taken pride in her ability to contain her emotions, to present her side of an argument with logic and clarity. Yet now the bubble of anger tightened her chest and disillusionment burned the back of her throat.

Earlier, he'd claimed that it hadn't been all bad, and she'd allowed herself a fleeting memory of the good. The stimulation she'd felt from conversations that ranged from wicked banter to sharp debate. The simple pleasure of walking beside him, the strength of his hand around hers, smiling when their strides fell into a matching rhythm. The more complex pleasure of his body joined with hers, delivering her to places unknown, to emotions unfelt.

She'd thought the aftermath, the consequences, his failure to respond to her phone calls, had destroyed all the good memories, but she'd been wrong. Some had lingered, enough for him to trample with today's insulting allegations. Enough that she now felt angry and bitter and profoundly disappointed in him and her own judgment.

Drawing a strengthening breath, she forced herself to face him one last time and to say what still needed to be said.

"I was about to tell you why I agreed when Mother suggested adding The Palisades to the marriage contract, but I will save my breath. It's obvious you don't remember anything about my character or my background or what we shared that weekend. I'm beginning to wonder if you remember me at all."

Suddenly she felt cold and drained and tired. She wanted home and the security of the choices she'd made, nice and orderly and safe. With strides that gathered strength and pace as she went, she circled the dining table and headed for the door.

He called her name, but she kept right on moving. When she heard the heavy pad of his footfalls against the timber floor, she moved even faster. Clumsy fingers struggled with the lock before, finally, she yanked the door open. But a large hand flattened against the timber beside her head and pushed it shut.

For a long second, she stared at the broad curve of his thumb, while her heart raced and her body registered the familiar heat and weight of his body at her back. Far too close, all too familiar. Anger welled up inside her, and this time, she welcomed its rescuing strength.

"Let me go," she said through gritted teeth.

"Not yet." His voice was low and conciliatory, his breath warm against the side of her face.

The traitorous response that prickled through Susannah's skin only made her madder. She refused to be taken in by false apologies or belated attempts at placation. She ungritted her teeth, but only so she could speak. "You have three seconds," she said tightly, "before I scream blue murder. If you remember nothing else, then you should remember how far my voice carries across this headland."

Closing her eyes, she started the count but only made it through one before the warmth of his breath distracted her. At two he started to speak; at three his words took hold.

"I don't remember, Susannah. You, your scream, anything."

Three

Stunned, Susannah peeled herself from the door and turned within the wide stance of his body. He didn't back off more than a few inches leaving her little room to manoeuvre. The impact of his words blurred with the shock of contact between his knees and her thighs, her elbow and his chest. Renewed heat bloomed beneath her skin, quick and unquenchable.

Squeezing her eyelids tight, she forced the memories—only memories, she told herself again—back under control so she could concentrate on the present. *His* memory, or lack thereof. But when she opened her eyes, her gaze caught on the broad vee of chest exposed between the gaping sides of his robe. The exposed skin, the sprinkle of dark hair, the line of raised flesh…

She sucked in an audible breath and without conscious thought, reached up to push the towelling aside. To reveal scar tissue that hadn't existed ten weeks ago. "My God, Donovan. What happened?"

When he didn't answer, she raised her stunned gaze and found his attention fixed on where her hand clutched the edge of his robe, the backs of her fingers resting flush against the heat of his skin. She released her grip, reclaimed her hand, and slowly his gaze shifted to her face, silvery eyes narrowed and aware. It was a look she recognised but didn't want to remember.

Without answering her question, he pushed away from the door and strolled back to the table where he'd abandoned the bottle of red wine earlier.

When he held up the bottle and raised an eyebrow in question, she nodded, and the familiarity of that silent exchange brought a confused frown to her face as she watched him pour two glasses.

I don't remember. You, your scream, anything.

"You don't remember… Is that because of what happened to cause the scar?" Her mind churned over his revelation and the possibilities. "Were you in an accident?"

"An accident, no. I was mugged." He gave a shrug, as if it were nothing. Or something he preferred others to see as nothing. "Woke up with a memory block."

Her gaze dropped to his chest, to the now-concealed scar. She had to moisten her dry mouth before she could speak. "And that?"

"One of their weapons, apparently, was a broken bottle."

With every appearance of complacency, he held

out the glass of wine he'd poured for her. Leaving the sanctuary of the door, Susannah managed to walk the dozen or so steps to take the proffered glass, despite the unsteadiness in her legs. Amazingly her voice sounded calm when she asked, "Where did this happen?"

"On my way home."

"You told me you don't have a home."

Surprise stilled the glass he'd been raising to his lips. It echoed briefly in his eyes before he answered. "I have a temporary home in San Francisco."

"When?"

Their eyes met over the rim of his glass and Susannah's racing heart skipped a beat, waiting, anticipating the answer. "In July. The day I returned from here."

"You were in hospital? Is that why—" She had to stop, to shake her head and clear the image of him broken and beaten from her mind's eye. "You didn't return my phone calls."

"Not until I returned to the office."

"How long was that?" she asked, her voice no longer even or steady.

"Two months, all up."

That's why he'd been constantly "unavailable" or "out of the office" over the weeks she'd tried to contact him. She'd assumed his assistant was screening his calls, that he'd chosen to ignore the messages, and she'd given up trying to get through.

Two months to recover from his injuries. My God.

Unable to master the trembling in her hand or legs, she put down the untouched drink and when Donovan pulled a chair from the table, she murmured her thanks and sank to its solid support. "That is a long time to be laid up."

"Tell me about it." He punctuated the wry response with the same hitch of his shoulder as before, a fake casualness that masked the tension etched in his face. For the first time since she'd watched him unobserved from the foyer of the gym, Susannah allowed herself to study him fully from head to foot. He looked so straight, so strong, so healthy. She didn't want to imagine the scale of injuries that would have kept him hospitalised for such an extended time.

"You look fit now," she said, when he caught her thorough inspection. She didn't need details of those injuries, she told herself. She didn't need to ask why his assistant had been so obstructively short with information. It was impossible to change what had happened and too late for regret. She needed to lighten the mood, to lift the crushing weight that had descended on her chest. "The punching bag I found you working over this morning—did that have the face of one of your attackers painted on it?"

A hint of amusement touched his lips as he took the chair next to hers. "Something along those lines."

"Did it help?"

"Not as much as hitting the real guy."

"You went down fighting?" Eyebrows arched in faux surprise, Susannah asked the question even though she knew the answer.

The day in July when he'd walked into her office unannounced, when she'd told him she wasn't available to take him to Stranger's Bay, warned her that he never gave up on anything without a fight. Then he'd set to work negotiating a price she couldn't turn down, talking her into dinner, seducing her with disarmingly direct words and the silvery smile of his eyes. She'd been charmed to the mat before the bell ended round one.

And now he'd returned to pursue the same fight, and a fight meant winners and losers. That foresight settled deep in her bones and when she lifted her gaze to Donovan's, all sign of amusement was gone.

"So I'm told," he said in response to her question about going down fighting. "I don't remember, but apparently I put one of them in hospital with me."

Although she strived, Susannah failed to keep the edge of dismay from her face. It didn't help that the chilling action played through her mind like a scene from a movie. Her gaze drifted up, to the shorter hair. Funny how that little detail hadn't really registered until now. "You were hit over the head?"

"And rendered unconscious," he confirmed, "thus ending the fight."

She nodded, swallowed. Her restless eyes shifted over him, searching out what else she may have missed, before returning to his eyes. "Do you remember *anything* from before the accident?"

"Everything, up until I left America. I remember bits and pieces of the days I spent in Melbourne. Meeting with the CEO at Horton Holdings. The hotel where I stayed. It was the Carlisle Grande," Van said with an unamused smile. Selected before he knew anything about Alex Carlisle and his family-owned group of hotels, other than he liked the beds and the service was impeccable.

"You don't remember coming here to Stranger's Bay that weekend?"

"No."

She shook her head and puffed out a short note of scepticism. "I thought amnesia only happened in books and movies."

Van's eyes narrowed on hers. "You think I'm making this up?"

In the pause, in the hint of a shrug, Van read her doubt. He jackknifed to his feet and stalked away a few paces.

"I believe you, I just find it so difficult to imagine not remembering anything."

That quietly spoken comment turned him back around. She sat straight and tall in the stiff-backed chair, her ivory coat still buttoned to the base of her throat. Against the rain-lashed windows, her hair was a bright splash of colour. Her eyes remained unsettled with a mixture of compassion and doubt.

It struck him like a blast of that rain-fuelled wind that he'd spent a whole weekend with her, here in these rooms. That coat he may well have unbuttoned and tossed aside. He might have stripped those boots from her legs. Kissed her in all the places that had drummed through his mind in those seconds he'd held her pinned against the door.

"I look at you sitting there," he said, his voice low and laced with the frustration of not knowing, "and I find it hard to believe that I don't remember you."

She blinked. A slow-motion movement of dark lashes against pale cheeks. "That must be a little...odd."

Van gave a hollow laugh. "There's one description."

"How have you dealt with it?"

He swirled the wine in his glass, wondering whether to answer. How much to share. But then he recalled the compassion in her eyes and, what the hell, he'd likely shared a whole lot more than this with Susannah Horton. "I talked to the people I was dealing with that week. I retraced my footsteps. I reconstructed. I cursed a lot."

"Cursing sometimes helps."

Van studied her sitting there all prim and proper in her buttoned-up coat, and he thought about her cursing in that crisp private-school voice. The image was intriguing. *She* was intriguing. "I have a business backer, a mentor, who believes curses are the spice of our bland language."

"Mac," she said softly.

Van's hand stilled and tightened around the stem of his wineglass. "I told you about her?"

"Yes, although there's no need to look so worried. You didn't let any family skeletons out of the closet, nor did I sneakily access the information from your possessions."

Although her words were flippant, there was a bite to her tone. He deserved it, and she deserved an apology. "I'm sorry that I insulted you with that insinuation. That wasn't my intention."

"Really? What was your intention?"

"To find out what had happened with the acquisition deal. When I left Melbourne, I had a deal on the table. When I woke up a week later, it was gone."

He saw a flicker of guilt and what could have been regret cross her face. If possible she blanched even more. "Telling me about your amnesia from the start would have made that conversation go a lot more smoothly."

"For you, yes."

"And you?"

Van met her eyes with unflinching directness. "I came here knowing *these* things about you, Susannah. You're Miriam Horton's daughter. I employed you to show me Stranger's Bay. You were engaged to Alex Carlisle."

"I wasn't en—"

"This is what I knew from your mother, and everyone I asked vouched for her integrity. But my point is," he stressed when she looked like interrupting, "I came here thinking the worst of you. If you'd known I remembered nothing, how could I have trusted anything you told me?"

"And now, do you believe anything I told you?"

"Yes."

Surprise widened her eyes and some colour returned to her face. She looked almost pleased, and Van felt a kick of satisfaction low in his gut, the kind that came from a surprise win on the markets or an unexpected victory at the negotiating table.

"Why?" she asked.

"Who could make up a story like that?"

Their eyes met and shared the dry humour of that answer in a rare moment of connection. Then wariness returned to chase away the smile. She stood suddenly, a quick, jerky movement at odds with her normal grace, and in the awkwardness he caught a distracting glimpse of knee, thigh, skirt. It was nothing overt, nothing sexual, but the sight threw him right off balance.

He'd seen that exact shift of motion before. It moved in and out of focus in the darkness that used to house his memory of that weekend.

"It doesn't make any difference, does it?"

Van looked up, the sensation gone in a blink, leaving him unsure if he'd remembered or only imagined remembering. "What doesn't?" he asked, frowning.

She lifted her hands and let them drop in a gesture of defeat. "Your amnesia—me now knowing about your accident—it changes nothing."

"Not even your perception of why I lost this acquisition?"

Her eyes clouded with an emotion Van hated. Pity. Sympathy. Compassion. Whatever label it wore, he'd seen enough these past ten weeks to last ten lifetimes. "I understand why you feel robbed and I'm very sorry, but that doesn't change what has happened since."

"One thing hasn't changed. I still want The Palisades. And after hearing why I lost out, I want it even more."

"I'm sorry," she said again, her voice rasping on the infernal word. "But it is too late. Can't you see that? The agreement has been made with Alex, the contract is drawn."

"But won't be signed until you marry Carlisle." He paused, swirling the last inch of red wine and allowing the idea that circled his brain to take root. "What happens to The Palisades sale if the marriage doesn't go ahead?"

"That is not going to happen," she said resolutely. "Alex is a man of this word. He will not pull out of this deal, no matter what you say or do. The threat you made about exposing our affair won't change his mind."

"And yet you came down here, presumably to stop me doing that."

"I came to find out what was going on, and why you

were back. Alex knows we weren't engaged that weekend, he knows I didn't cheat or lie to him, so he won't change his mind about marrying me."

"And what if *you* change your mind?"

"You're suggesting that *I* break my engagement?"

"We're not talking about a love match, Susannah. This is a business contract. You've been bartered like a high-price commodity."

A shadow crossed her face, but a spark of vehemence lit her eyes and lifted her chin. "Perhaps I wasn't clear earlier, but you're reading this wrong. Yes, this is an unusual alliance and it is bound and tied up like a business deal, but there was no coercion involved. I want to marry Alex. From this union I am getting everything I want. A husband I respect and admire, children, an extended family, as well as all the advantages being a Carlisle will bring to my business.

"I'm sorry, Donovan," she said drawing herself up tall. "I really am, but there is nothing I or you or anyone can do to change what's transpired. I really have to go now or this flight will leave without me, but when I get back to civilisation I will talk to Alex. He's a fair man. Perhaps he will reconsider that part of the contract."

His eyes narrowed. "I thought you said he wouldn't back down."

"I don't believe he will, but I'm offering to try. That's all I can do, other than suggest some other properties that would suit your purposes just as well as The Palisades."

"I'm not interested in another property. I came here to buy this one."

"Then I guess it's up to Alex."

* * *

"Not if I can help it," Van told himself after she'd left. He always steered his own ship. No way was he leaving his destiny in the hands of a competitor. Alex Carlisle might be a fair man, but he was also a business-man with a reputation for smart dealing.

Why would he give up The Palisades?

Sure, sweetheart, I'll tear up the contract so your last lover can have another shot at a prime property.

No, that was not going to happen. Carlisle wanted the property; he wanted Susannah as his wife; why the hell would he give up either?

From his terrace, Van tracked the careful progress of the resort's courtesy pickup as it schlooshed a wet path back to the central resort buildings. It had picked her up from his door, presumably to transport her to the helipad and her four-o'clock departure. Van couldn't see her going anywhere in this weather. In the hour since he'd stepped from the tub, the squalls of wind had grown flukier, the rain heavier.

The fact that she wasn't leaving—that she couldn't scurry back to the fiancé she respected and admired—did nothing to ease Van's darkening discontent. It was a tangle of frustration, of missed opportunity, of all she'd told him and all he didn't yet know.

Hands braced on the balcony railing, he glared out into a landscape tailor-made for his mood. Past the dark jut of the clifftop, he could just make out the churn of whitecaps against the obsidian waters of the bay. Some-where out there, shielded by the thickening curtain of rain, sat Charlotte Island. The private and exclusive island was the heart of the resort property and the reason no substitute would do.

He would have visited in July, he had no doubt about that despite his lack of memories or photographs. Both were lost to the chance of fate that put him the same place at the same time as that trio of brawny thieves. They'd taken more than his possessions, they'd also stolen a chunk of precious time.

He slapped his hand down against the steel rail as a bead of suppressed fury exploded inside him.

With every week he'd been laid up mending broken bones and bruised organs, Mac had slipped another week closer to the end. Now, more than ever, he wanted this land returned to her ownership. His last and only meaningful gift to the woman who'd shaped him from a cocky young upstart to a respected equity player.

Lifting his face to the icy kiss of the rain, he considered his options. He could tell Susannah why he was set on acquiring this land. Maybe that would stir sufficient sympathy for his cause, maybe she would even talk to Carlisle as she'd promised, but compassion was not recognised currency in the cut-throat world of business. And no matter how many ways she cried family-husband-happiness, this marriage was a business arrangement.

Bottom line, he had one chance—and one night—to buy himself back into this deal.

All he had to do was stop the wedding from going ahead.

Four

"Listen to that rain! I bet you're glad you decided to stay."

The reservations manager came out of the bathroom where she'd been checking to ensure Susannah had all the necessary toiletries. Since she'd left home with nothing but a hastily packed tote bag, she was grateful for whatever the resort could supply for her unexpected overnight stay.

Before she could respond to Gabrielle's comment, the drumming of rain on the villa's iron roof intensified to a deafening din. Susannah closed her mouth. She might not be exactly glad about staying, but the weather had robbed her of any choice.

Gabrielle joined her in the bedroom, her nose creasing into a wince as she gazed out the window. "We made the right decision in talking you out of driving."

By *we* she meant the resort staff. Susannah had been all for leaving by whatever means available. With the helicopter shuttle grounded, she'd asked about hiring a car—heck, she'd even offered to buy a four-wheel drive belonging to Jock, the doorman-cum-resort-chauffeur! But everyone from Jock to the manager had declared her crazy to consider attempting the long drive in such hazardous conditions.

Watercraft had been suggested as an "if you absolutely must leave" option, and Susannah shuddered. There was a line between absolutely-need-to and really-want-to, and that line was the wide expanse of choppy waves between here and Appleton.

"You'll be comfortable here for tonight." Gabrielle finished plumping the massed arrangement of pillows on the bed and straightened. "And if the worst comes to the worst, we will look into the boat option tomorrow."

"Is there a possibility the shuttle won't be flying?" Susannah asked on a rising note of concern.

"I trust it won't come to that." The other woman's cheerful smile was spoiled by a flicker of concern in her eyes. "I am sorry I couldn't put you in your usual accommodation. Unfortunately our other guest had already reserved The Pinnacle."

"There's no need to apologise, Gabrielle. I didn't have a reservation and you've known me long enough to realise that I never expect deferential treatment just because of my name."

"I know, but thank you for the reassurance. It's been quite a day."

"It has," Susannah agreed. *And it wasn't over yet.*

Her heart kicked up a beat, recalling the wording Gabrielle had used. "Did I hear you correctly when you referred to 'the other guest'? Are there just the two of us here tonight?"

"We had a late cancellation due to the weather, from a group who'd booked most of the resort for a corporate team-building exercise."

"Is the forecast that bad?"

"For beach games and bushwalking?" Gabrielle's smile was wry when she tilted her head as if listening to the remorseless rain. "I'd say, yes."

For *anything* outdoors, Susannah conceded as she studied the view—or lack thereof—from the bedroom window. Her thoughts zeroed to the only other guest and his intentions. Why had he come back to Stranger's Bay? Was he really reconstructing that weekend?

Her pulse thudded. Her gaze skimmed over the bed and a vivid memory of how they'd spent much of their weekend flared low in her belly.

She chased it away with a reminder of where she was supposed to be tonight and the heat turned chill.

"Is there anything wrong with your bed?" Gabrielle sounded puzzled. "If you require more pillows, or a specific—"

"No, no," Susannah said quickly. "I was miles away, thinking about something else entirely. I had a…date… for tonight."

"I'm sure he'll understand."

Susannah wasn't so sure, but she followed Gabrielle out to the state-of-the-art kitchen where the other woman continued her check of the pantry and refrigerator. "The basics are all here but I'll order a hamper from catering and send it along once the rain eases. As for dinner—"

"Please, don't go to any more trouble on my behalf," Susannah implored. "I'm sure the hamper will be more than enough without ordering in dinner."

Gabrielle made her way to the door. "You know nothing is ever too much trouble. If you change your mind or if there's anything else you need, I'm a phone call away. And if there's any update on the weather or transport, I will let you know."

"I would appreciate that. Thank you."

After Susannah closed the door, she roamed from room to room, contemplating the ramifications of being stranded here longer than overnight. In an effort at optimism, she told herself this would delay facing the wrath of Alex for another day. Unfortunately that couldn't dispel the ominous downside—she and Donovan Keane were here alone.

Knowing he was ensconced in the luxurious villa where they'd shared that other weekend left her feeling restless and uneasy. It was a sensation she understood far too well. From the moment she first met Donovan Keane, he'd unsettled her senses and her equilibrium.

Even now, with the curtain of rain adding an extra layer of isolation to each of the scattered villas, she felt his presence in every overly responsive female cell.

Paused at the window facing out toward the bay, she lifted her hands to rub the goose bumps that had sprung up on her arms. She needed warm. She needed dry. But first she needed a long, hot shower.

When she exited the steam-shrouded bathroom a half hour later, her hair wrapped turban-style in a towel, she felt toasty warm and as relaxed as possible given the robe was identical to the one Donovan had worn. She hung her clothes on the dining chairs and thought about lighting the fire. The more quickly they dried, the more quickly she could shed this reminder of Donovan.

Unconsciously her hand came up to clutch the lapel, and her stomach tightened again with the shock of that moment of discovery. The scar, his story, her imagining of his injuries.

A knock at the door startled her out of her introspection.

Her first thought—*it's him!*—gave way to a deprecating huff of breath. It would be catering with the promised hamper. Her nerves breathed a sigh of relief and her stomach rumbled in anticipation. She'd missed lunch and the airline breakfast had been insubstantial and too long ago.

"Just a second," she called, unpeeling the towel from her hair. Skirting the makeshift laundry, she hurried to the door. And where she should have seen a uniformed member of the resort's catering staff smiling a greeting, she saw Donovan Keane leaning against the door frame.

Dressed in dark trousers and a white shirt, he looked hauntingly familiar. Just like their first night here at Stranger's Bay when he'd appeared uninvited on her doorstep.

As he straightened, the silver drift of his gaze took her all in, from the tips of her bare toes to the top of her tangled curls. All the blood drained from Susannah's brain into her skin. Annoyance and agitation and dismay warred with those unruly female responses.

Stop it, she warned her hormones. *You do not want to see him. Especially straight from the shower with no underwear, no makeup, no defences.*

"What are you doing here?" she asked curtly.

He inclined his head, indicating a hefty picnic-style hamper at his feet. "Dinner, I hope."

Taking advantage of Susannah's slackjawed surprise, Van picked up the weighty basket and brushed past her.

She recovered enough to catch at his shirtsleeve. "Stop. Wait."

If he'd wanted, Van could have shrugged off that attempt to stop his entry. Instead he paused a step inside the door and half a step from her flushed countenance. For the first time, he noticed the scatter of freckles on her nose, visible because her face was scrubbed clean from the shower.

His gaze dipped to her throat and then to her chest. Barely visible beneath the rosy tint of her skin, more of those freckles spanned the deep V created by the wraparound garment. He would wager his entire portfolio of blue chips that she wore nothing underneath…nothing but a blush and that faint sprinkle of gold-dust freckles.

He noted the rapid beat of pulse at the base of her throat, and her hand released his sleeve to clutch the robe tight across her breasts. Slowly his gaze lifted to her face. He'd placed her at a distinct disadvantage turning up unannounced, and that's exactly what he'd hoped to do.

Catering had delivered his hamper of provisions first

and, in an idle conversation about the weather, the waiter named Rogan revealed that his second and only other port of call was, "A day visitor caught out by the storm. Chopper's grounded so she had to stay the night."

Van's plan had formulated in a fortuitous heartbeat.

To avoid a drenching he'd hitched a ride with Rogan in the catering van, and along the way he'd planned his approach. Patience, finesse, play that compassion he'd glimpsed in her eyes earlier. He hadn't considered that he might enjoy himself in the process.

Looking down at her now, at the tremble in her slender fingers as they held the sides of her robe together, at the nervous swipe of her tongue as she moistened her lips, Van knew he was going to enjoy this far more than he had any right to. He reached past her wet tumble of curls and leaned his weight against the still-open door. Apparently her grip on the doorknob matched her one on the robe. He applied more pressure until her death grip gave and the door closed with a muffled click. Although the wicker hamper provided a safe barrier between their bodies, she flattened herself against the cedar door as if she wanted nothing more than to slink inside it.

Suppressing a smile, Van eased his weight off the door. Earlier, when he'd held her captive against another door, he hadn't indulged himself with anything more than breathing her scent. This time, he selected one tightly spiralled curl and tucked it behind her ear, deliberately brushing her cheek with the knuckle of his middle finger.

Her skin was as silky soft as the sound of her indrawn breath, as warm as the response cutting through his veins.

"What do you think you're doing?" she asked in a pitchy rush. Worry carved a frown into the space between her perfectly shaped eyebrows.

"Don't worry, Susannah." He gave her a wolfish smile, and just for the hell of it touched his fingertips to that frown. "I'm here to eat dinner, not you."

He left her there, all wide-eyed shock and open-mouthed indignation, and strolled to the kitchen portion of the open-plan living space. He hefted the hamper onto the countertop and started unpacking the contents.

"Why?"

Van looked up. He hadn't heard her bare-footed approach, but he noticed how she carefully skirted the island counter, keeping its solid width between them. He noticed that her cheekbones were still tinged with pink.

"Why what?" he asked, inspecting the label on a local Gewürztraminer, before putting the bottle down. He looked into the wary distrust of her eyes. "Why am I eating dinner, or why aren't I eating—"

"Why are you *here*. And why did you bring my supplies instead of catering?"

"Rogan was doing the delivery but I took pity on the poor man, running about in the rain."

"Didn't he have a vehicle?" she asked.

"Yes, but it isn't easy keeping dry." Van's gaze shifted to the room beyond her, to where the articles of her clothing hung on every available piece of furniture. "It would appear you had a similar problem."

"*You* managed."

"Ah, but I'm quick."

"Not al—"

She stopped, her lips compressing into a tight line. Van went still. "Not al-*ways*?" he ventured.

Oh, yeah. That's what she'd been about to let slip. The truth swirled in her eyes even as she shook her head. The notion of a long, lazy exploration of those long legs and freckles ambushed his brain for a sweet second...

"I was going to say that not all the staff would care about getting a bit damp."

Van had to admire her quick improvisation.

"I wouldn't have thought Rogan would mind," she continued. "I believe we're the only two guests, so he hasn't exactly got a lot of running around to do."

"Since we are the only guests, I suggested he go home." He unearthed a corkscrew from the well-stocked utensils drawer and looked up enquiringly. "Which wine shall I open, the red or the white?"

A frown creased her brow as she looked from one bottle to the other, then she drew an audible breath. "Look, Donovan, I really don't think this is a good idea."

"Why not? Don't you trust yourself to share dinner with me?"

"It's *you* I don't trust," she fired back. "You invited yourself here without any forewarning, and I know it has nothing to do with dinner or sparing Rogan from extra work. You always have an agenda."

"And what agenda do you think I'm pursuing here, apart from dinner, company and conversation?"

"The one that brought you to Stranger's Bay in the first place. An eight-figure deal you spent a lot of resources working on, and that you don't appreciate losing."

"There are a lot of things I don't appreciate losing,

Susannah," he said mildly, but there was nothing mild in his gaze. "Especially when the fight isn't fair."

"I understand why you might feel that way, but—"

"Do you? Do you understand what it's like to lose days from your life? To not know what you'd said, what you'd done, what you'd shared?"

Her gaze glittered under his for a moment, before falling away.

"I figure we shared dinner, company and conversation that weekend in a villa just like this one." He applied himself to opening the Gewürztraminer while he selected his words and their casual delivery for maximum effect. "Your fiancé can hardly complain about the circumstances that have been thrust upon you. You said he's a fair man. Would he object to you joining me at the dinner table and helping me recover something of what I've lost?"

"Helping you…how?" she asked after a moment, her voice edged with wariness.

"You asked how I was dealing with this memory blank. I told you I'd worked on backtracking, gathering information, recreating events. I've put everything together…everything except those days here."

"I'm sorry, Donovan. I can't do that. I can't help you recreate that weekend."

"I'm only asking you to talk to me, to share some of where we went, what we did." He poured a splash of the pale golden wine into a glass and slid it across the countertop. "You can tell me where we ate, what we drank."

He could see her vacillating, her gaze uneasy, the infinitesimal slump in her shoulders as her willpower weakened. Reaching forward he touched his index finger to the back of her hand. Just that one touch to bring her uneasy gaze winging back to his.

"You might not be able to help me with anything else I lost, but you can help me with this."

Although she didn't answer straight away, he saw the capitulation in her expressive green eyes. Satisfaction churned rich and strong through his blood, but he waited, his posture deceptively casual while she prepared her answer.

"I can try." She lifted her chin a notch. "But I want to make it clear that all I'm providing are the facts."

"That's all I expect."

"I can't promise to remember everything."

"I'm sure you remember the important things."

Her gaze fell away, and she lifted a hand to rub at her upper arm. Cold...or nervous? "We can talk over dinner, but afterward I have things to do."

"Hair to wash, laundry to do," Van murmured. She'd already swung away to gather up the clothes scattered around the table. A pink skirt and white sweater. Lacy white bra. A wisp of nothing that had to be underwear.

She held them all tight to her chest as she faced him across the table, clearly unamused by his aside. "I have phone calls to make."

To Carlisle, Van guessed. *The man who'd won what he had lost.*

That thought killed the buzz of warm satisfaction he'd had going. The touch of mean left in its place wouldn't let him watch her scurry off with her armful of clothes without one last bite. "You don't have to change on my account. I imagine I've seen you in a robe before…and without."

At the door to her bedroom, she paused to cut him a disparaging look. "That is precisely the reason I suggested this dinner was a bad idea."

"Because I've seen you naked?"

Colour flared in her cheekbones, but her eyes remained cool and steady on his. "Because I can't trust you not to mention that fact."

"And that makes you uncomfortable?"

"I'm engaged to marry another man. Of course it does."

As if Van needed that reminder. Or that extra jab to his prickly mood. "Do you think I would try to seduce another man's bride?" he asked.

"I think you would do whatever it takes to get your hands on the contract to The Palisades."

With the hair dryer on high, Susannah blasted the remaining dampness from her clothes before turning the appliance on her hair. That was a necessity, not a vanity. Plus it ate up some time while she worked on her composure. Perhaps if she remained locked in the bathroom long enough, her "guest" would go away and leave her to regret past mistakes in peace.

Or perhaps not.

She allowed her memory to slide briefly to that weekend, to recall an exchange where she'd described him as a can-do man. With an amused grin he'd shaken his head and said, "No. I'm more *will-do*."

She didn't allow herself to dwell on the memory of how he'd demonstrated that *will-do* quality. Instead she used the knowledge to bolster her defences. She had agreed to help him out because she did sympathise over his lost memory and the circumstances that had led him to lose the deal.

But it was only a deal. He would get over that loss and move on to another deal, another property, another asset. Alex did not have the luxury of that time. He needed a wife now, and The Palisades was part of that marriage contract.

Tonight's dinner was only about helping Donovan fill in some blanks in his memory. She could do that. And she could do it while remaining cool and calm and not letting him get to her with his incendiary taunts.

She was not going to let him forget that she was another man's bride.

Leaning back from the mirror she studied herself in the unforgiving light and crinkled her nose. Not exactly the picture of cool, calm and collected that she was aiming for. Despite her best efforts, her hair had taken on a life of its own. A pulse beat noticeably at the base of her throat. Her skin remained rosy-pink from the blow-drying.

Well, at least the colour matched her skirt.

With a last wry grimace at her reflection, she padded through to the bedroom. Wet boots or bare feet? Stitched-up composure or comfort? Dithering over that choice she heard the low rumble of his voice from beyond her closed door.

Perhaps the storm was easing. Perhaps salvation had arrived.

Discarding the boots, she hurried back to the living

area only to find Donovan as alone as she'd left him. The microwave whirred busily at his back. The table was set. He looked up from slicing what looked and smelled like a homemade sourdough loaf. "Hungry?"

Susannah ignored her stomach's growling response and the unsettling notion of how comfortable he looked in her kitchen. "Did I hear you speaking to someone just then?"

"Phone." He pointed out the instrument across the living room with the wickedly serrated knife. "It was Gabrielle. A courtesy call to check the food had arrived and that everything was to your satisfaction."

She glanced at the dishes he'd set out on the table, and nodded. Of course the food would be better than satisfactory—it was one of The Palisades' premium selling points. "Did she mention the transport situation?"

"Yes, but the news is not what you wanted to hear. The helicopter won't be back until Monday at the earliest."

A sick feeling of dread tightened Susannah's throat. "The weather forecast is that dire?"

"The forecast isn't bad, but the rain was even heavier and more prolonged farther south. There's flooding over a widespread area and the chopper used for this service has been seconded for rescue operations." He looked up from his bread cutting and met her eyes. "Since we're safe and dry here, I suggested that we could wait until after the emergencies."

"Do you mean we're stuck here indefinitely?"

"Gabrielle mentioned a charter service they use for day trips. If the sea settles, it can ferry us across the bay," he said with irritating calm. While he spoke, he carried the bread and whatever he'd nuked in the microwave to the table, depositing both alongside a bowl of salad. He held out a chair, inviting her to sit. "You might as well make yourself comfortable."

Stiff-backed and a long way from comfortable, Susannah slid into the chair. She took extra care to avoid contact with the hands resting casually against its back. "For how long?" she asked, her voice husky with nerves.

"A day or two, at most." He took his place across the table, the glint in his eyes as silvery sharp as the knife he'd wielded before. A shiver tracked her spine like the trickle of raindrops on glass as he slowly smiled. "But who knows? It's in the hands of the Gods. Why don't you relax and enjoy?"

Five

Relax and enjoy? I don't think so.

But when Susannah watched him ladle a generous serving of chowder-style soup into her bowl, her stomach decided that, yes, it could very-much enjoy. The dish was as good as it looked and smelled, and with the edge taken from her hunger she was able to relax enough to see the positive side of her situation.

As long as they couldn't leave, no one could arrive. And the only thing worse than being trapped here alone with Donovan Keane, was being *discovered* trapped here alone with Donovan Keane by, for example, Alex. He hadn't called and her mother hadn't called back, either. She'd expected to hear from someone...unless the phones were out.

"Did Gabrielle mention the phone lines being down?"

He looked up from buttering a slice of bread. "No. Why do you ask?"

"I just wondered, with all the rain, and mine has been so silent." She cast a glance in that direction, then sat up straight as it struck her that— "I didn't hear it ring earlier."

"Above that wailing hair dryer?"

Point taken, but still… "It's strange that Gabrielle didn't mention the flooding when I spoke to her. She seemed quite optimistic about tomorrow."

"Are you suggesting I fabricated her phone call?" he asked after a long beat of consideration. He set down his knife and leaned back in his chair, his hooded gaze inscrutable. "To what end?"

"To keep me here," Susannah replied, mimicking his deliberate intonation.

"Kidnapping? Isn't that a little extreme?"

Despite the lazy amusement in his voice, the weight of his steady gaze made her heart beat a little faster, a little harder. And her earlier words resonated in the thickening silence between them.

You would do whatever it takes to get your hands on the contract to The Palisades.

"What lengths do you think I would go to," he said conversationally, "to keep you here? Would I use restraint, for example?"

"Hypothetically speaking, I would pick blackmail or some other form of verbal coercion as more your speed. You're far too clever with your tongue to need to use physical force or restraint."

For a long moment he studied her in silence, and the warmth of a flush rose unbidden in her face. And she silently berated herself for allowing him to lead her down this path. It was too suggestive, too sensually alluring.

"Now you've gone and aroused my curiosity." Leaning forward, he captured her gaze and held it in place with the silky restraint of his tone. "We never got kinky then? I didn't have to tie you up to have my wicked way with you?"

"I was willing."

"Past tense."

"Absolutely."

His lips tilted at one corner in the sexy half smile that had rendered her willing on so many occasions. He picked up his wine and there was the hint of a salute in the gesture, as if he appreciated her candid responses. But there was a different appreciation in his eyes, one she should not be enjoying, but it was also a challenge from which she couldn't back down.

"Now—present tense—if I wanted to keep you here I might need to tie you up. Toss you on that boat Gabrielle mentioned. Take you out to the island."

Susannah pretended to give that some thought. "How proficient are you with a captive who's prone to brutal seasickness?"

One eyebrow quirked. "I take it that's not a hypothetical?"

"Unfortunately, no."

"Then I'll take that into account, should I ever wish to abduct you."

"I'd appreciate that." With a serene smile, she tilted her face toward his plate. "Are you finished with your first course?"

She removed their plates, and on her way to the kitchen, she could feel him tracking her every step of the way. Her heart continued to beat too fast and the tight heat in her skin was *so* not good, but she liked the intensity of sensation. She'd forgotten how much she liked the word play, the eye play, the play of his smile. She'd forgotten how one simple exchange with this man could turn her self-perception from cool, cautious and composed to smart, sharp and sexy.

And it was wrong. Already she had indulged herself far more than she had any right to.

She shut the dishwasher on their first-course plates with an audible snap and returned to the table, to the safe and sensible second-course salad.

"I'm intrigued by the boat thing," he said.

Susannah's stomach dipped as if she'd stepped from land onto a moving deck, but she didn't look up from her plate. "Why is that?"

"With your job in the travel industry, I thought you'd be an expert on all means of transportation."

"I book them," she told him. "I don't have to do them. Besides, travel is only one part of At Your Service."

"The other parts being?"

"Whatever a client wants, we'll find it. Travel, transport, accommodation, entertainment, shopping, staff."

"Is that how you met Carlisle?" he asked. "Through your business?"

Susannah so did not want to go there, but what could she do? Return to banter about abduction and bondage? She'd promised conversation and it stood to reason that the conversation would circle on back to the common conflict. Alex Carlisle, her marriage contract, his business contract.

She took a sip of her wine and placed the glass carefully on the table. "Yes and no. We'd crossed paths many times at business and social events over the years, and when I started my own business, those connections were vital. My early growth was all word-of-mouth and making myself known to the people who could provide the level of service my clients require. Last year, I entered into an alliance with Carlisle Hotels."

"They scratch your back, you scratch theirs?"

The cool note in his voice stilled the play of Susannah's fingers on her wineglass and steadied her gaze on his. She lifted her chin a fraction. "Only when it best serves a client's needs."

"The Carlisle hotels have their own concierges."

"Yes, but my service is at another level. Sometimes they bring me in to help at a hotel level or they recommend a client contact me directly for a specific or unusual request."

His eyes thinned with an expression she recognised, and she braced herself for another of those disparaging remarks. Possibly about Alex's specific request for a wife. But whatever he'd been thinking, remained unsaid. He took another drink from his wine.

"Why personal concierging?" he asked.

"It plays to my strengths."

"Which are?"

"A known name, a lifetime's knowledge of the lux market and a BlackBerry filled with excellent contacts."

"That would be the flip answer, but you're serious

about your business. Otherwise you wouldn't be working so hard to save it."

Although he lazed back in his chair, his tone as casual as his posture, Susannah sensed real interest. In her, the woman, not the conduit to his own ambition.

Careful, she warned herself as her body warmed to that interest. *Don't be fooled by those silver eyes and tongue.*

"It's important because it's mine," she said simply, although the truth behind that answer was not so simple. "I conceived it, I chased capital to start it, its success or failure is all down to me."

"You believe you can succeed in such a specialist field with a limited pond of possible clients?"

"That's my point of difference," she said, leaning forward as she latched on to her favourite topic. "My target clientele isn't limited to the billionaire market. At Your Service is available to anyone, for any service, not only the big-dollar extravagances that anyone can buy with the right-sized cheque."

"The everyman concierge service?"

He sounded dubious and Susannah smiled as she conceded his point. "Okay, so not quite 'every' man. Most of my clients are either professionals with stacked schedules or visiting executives with the same time challenge. My job isn't only providing specific requests but also accessing what the client *really* wants…even when he or she doesn't know exactly what that might be."

"For example?"

"A place like Stranger's Bay. The experience is the isolation and the wild beauty, it's the escape from civilisation without feeling uncivilised. Every whim is catered but not in an obvious fashion. The staff, the service, everything is first-rate and discreet. That appeals to one client, while another wants staff on tap and constant pampering. My strength is in knowing which experience matches each client."

"Your strength is in looking after other people's needs," he suggested.

She smiled right back at him and said, "Yes. I guess it is."

There was an honesty in that moment, a connection that lasted a long moment before she remembered that this is what she'd warned herself about earlier. Not once, *but twice.* Yet again she'd stumbled into the dangerous trap of sharing too much, feeling too much and responding too easily to the wrong man.

Dinner was over. It was time to return to the real world.

Under the guise of clearing the table, she started to stand, but he stilled her with a hand on her arm. "Leave it. Stay and talk."

"I can't."

Her words were barely audible above the pounding of her heart. He rose to his feet and using that hot encircling grip on her wrist, he drew her around the table. "You can," he said. "You said you would tell me the important things."

"I said I would try," Susannah corrected, as inch by inch, he urged her nearer. With nothing to anchor her, she couldn't resist, could do nothing but hold herself tall and stiff as the steely heat of his hand permeated her skin and raced through her blood.

She came to a halt toe to toe with his black leather

loafers. In bare feet, she barely reached his chin and that put her eyes on a level with the open neck of his shirt. She felt ridiculously weak, even before he slackened his hold and let his palm slide up to her elbow and back to take her hand in his.

"Is this the part you thought you'd have trouble remembering accurately?" His words sloughed against her temple; their meaning swirled with liquid desire low in her belly. "Because when I get this close to you, I can't believe that anything we did together would be forgettable."

Susannah hadn't forgotten. *Anything.* Including the reason she shouldn't be standing here thinking about touching him. Thinking about kissing him.

Lifting her free hand to his chest, she pushed until he had to let her go. "This is the part I won't let myself remember," she said. "Now, I think you should go."

"You have phone calls to make."

Susannah nodded. "I do. If I'm going to be away more than overnight, there are people I need to let know."

"Family?"

"My sister. Half sister," she corrected herself. "And my neighbour. She worries." She folded her fingers into her palm, trapping his heat there. It was a small thing to keep of him, but all she would allow. "Good night, Donovan."

He surprised her by turning to go, then he stopped and turned back. "If you're thinking of calling Gabrielle, she's off duty tonight. She said you're welcome to call anytime, regardless. Front office has the number."

"Thank you, but I won't bother her at home. I know she will call if there are any further developments."

"You don't want to verify my story?"

"I believe you. Who could make up a story like that?"

It was supposed to be tongue-in-cheek, a reference to his comment about believing her convoluted explanation of how the deal on The Palisades had become tied up in her marriage contract. But after the door closed behind him, after she'd packed away the remains of their dinner and tried calling Alex, Zara, Alex's brother Rafe, then the suite at the Melbourne Carlisle Grande where she and Alex should have been staying tonight— the only person who picked up was her mother, and at least she promised to call Alex—she had nothing left to do but think.

And her thoughts were all an eddying whirl of Donovan Keane.

Did she trust him? On the transportation issue, yes. It was a story she could easily check with the resort staff or the company which ran the helicopter shuttle.

Did she trust him in a wider sense? No. Although she had to give him props for not taking advantage of the moment when he'd pulled her close. He could have kissed her. He could have insisted on staying, he could have pushed her for intimate details of their weekend activities. But he'd left almost too easily and without any goodbye, which made her more suspicious and more intrigued.

Was that his intention?

Standing at the scenic window looking out into the night, the dark shiver deep in Susannah's flesh was part chill, part apprehension. She couldn't stop her mind turning over the possibilities of why he'd accepted the end to the evening with such uncharacteristic compliance. Their dinner couldn't have helped his memory a great deal. It couldn't have furthered his need to reconstruct the lost weekend.

Yes, they'd covered some of the same conversational ground as last time but he hadn't pushed for specific details or asked the did-we-do-this, did-we-eat-that questions she'd anticipated. She understood his need to know, and she understood the kind of man he was—the kind who needed all the facts, the kind who controlled his own life, the kind who didn't give up.

Those missing days had to be like a burr digging into his psyche. She'd feared he would be unrelenting; that when he'd taken her hand and pulled her close to the tempting heat of his body, he would keep on in a relentless quest for details of how the seduction went down. So to speak.

Intimate memories whispered through her skin and she leaned closer to the window and pressed her overheated cheek against the cool glass. Why hadn't he pressed for more? Why had he let her go without taking advantage?

Perhaps tonight had been only the start. Perhaps she would wake tomorrow to find him on her doorstep again, this time with breakfast. Perhaps he would use their isolation and her growing restlessness and the compassion she felt for his situation to chip away at her resolve until he'd exposed every secreted emotion from its hiding place.

Looking out into the pitch-black night, she realised that the rain had stopped and the resulting quiet felt almost eerie in its intensity. The aloneness, the isolation, crept out of that quiet like Donovan's thieves, catching her unawares. If he'd arrived at her door right then, he would have found her exposed and vulnerable to anything that eased the choking grip of loneliness.

Dangerous thoughts.

Susannah pushed away from the window to prowl the confines of her villa. She was honest enough to recognise that danger, in herself and in her responses to Donovan. He had a way of making her feel a curious combination of strength and weakness, of safety and insecurity, of knowing what she wanted yet fearing everything that exposed.

She had to get away. She had to get back to Alex and the sanctuary of a future that answered all her needs. Tomorrow if—please, God!—the rain had really stopped.

Do you want to escape badly enough to get on the boat Gabrielle offered?

She paused by the window and thought about all she'd risked by coming here today. She'd let down Alex, her mother, everything that mattered.

Yes, she would brave the boat trip. Heck, if somebody strapped her into a canoe and handed her the oar, she would paddle like a crazy woman all the way home.

It's only a boat, she told herself. Just a short trip across the bay. How bad could that be?

"I've never known a punctual woman who was worth knowing, so I'm willing to wait another five minutes."

"This one's worth knowing," Van assured the owner of

the charter boat, who'd introduced himself as Gilly. "My guess—if she's not here by eleven, then she's not coming."

"Your call," Gilly said affably. "Just holler when you're ready to cast off."

He jumped back on board—nimbly for a man the size of a linebacker—and disappeared inside. The luxury motor cruiser was more boat than Van had expected but Gilly explained that his business was geared more toward fishing and pleasure charters than today's impromptu ferry trip to the nearest town across the bay.

Van assumed Susannah would have a car arranged and waiting to take her to the airport and her flight home to Melbourne.

Arms folded across his chest, he scanned the hillside that rose steeply toward the resort. She'd told the desk staff she would make her own way down to the jetty, but now he wondered if she'd chickened out. The tone of last night's exchange about seasickness might have been teasing, but he sensed she'd not been kidding about her aversion to boats.

But if she wanted to leave here badly enough…

A now-familiar flash of colour bobbing in and out of sight on the hillside path brought his musing up short. Not the bright yellow umbrella but the sheen of red-gold hair. Behind him Van heard the thump of Gilly's feet as he landed on the timber pier. He hmphed in satisfaction. "That looks like our other passenger now."

Van didn't answer. His attention remained fixed on Susannah, his heartbeat thickening as he anticipated the moment when she caught sight of him. He'd imagined his presence would be a surprise, and he wasn't wrong.

Her stride faltered infinitesimally. Her head came up. Her fingers tightened on the tote bag slung over her shoulder.

Then Gilly called out a greeting and she straightened her shoulders and stepped onto the timber planks of the jetty. She wore the same coat as yesterday, the same boots, but there was something different about her, Van mused, studying her approach with narrowed interest. When a sudden snap of breeze grabbed at her hair, she lifted a hand to push it back into order and he was struck by another minibolt of déjà vu.

It was the wind in her hair. Or the sun lighting it in a dozen shades of gold. Or the way she caught the bright mass all together and held it at the side of her throat, bunched in one hand.

Whatever it was, he'd seen it before. The first instances he'd discounted as insignificant, but not anymore. Just being around her tapped into that deep well of forgotten moments, and that made another good case for keeping her close.

Straightening from the mooring he'd been leaning against, he greeted her with a lazy smile. "Good morning, Susannah. Enjoying the sunshine?"

Designer sunglasses obscured half her face but they didn't disguise the pique in her voice. "What are you doing here?"

"Same as you, I expect."

"You're leaving today?"

"Can't see much point in staying," he said, "once you've gone."

Gilly cleared his throat, a reminder of his presence

and a reminder that they needed to get going. "Morning, Miss Horton. If you're ready, I'll help you aboard. Is that all your luggage?"

"Yes. I—"

"I'll help Susannah," Van said smoothly. Then to Gilly, "You have to admire a woman who travels this light."

Her lips tightened ominously but when she didn't fire back the expected salvo, Van took a closer look and realised that she wasn't only surprised at finding him here or angry that he'd hijacked her attempt to escape him. Against the dark frames of her glasses and under the clear September sky, her skin looked even paler than yesterday, that gold-dust sprinkling of freckles more pronounced. And the fingers gripping the leather straps of her bag reflected the same tension he saw in the tight set of her lips.

His smile faded. "You really do have a thing about boats, don't you?"

"Only about getting on them," she muttered. Then her shoulders went back and her nostrils flared as if she'd drawn a swift breath. Deftly, she stepped around him and allowed Gilly to hand her on board.

Van intercepted before she reached the cabin, and steered her toward the flydeck. At the base of the steps she dug in her heels. "I would prefer to sit inside."

"Your stomach won't thank you," he said mildly.

"I've taken something for that."

"You got the Dramamine then?"

"How did you know...?" Beneath his hand, he felt her stiffen. She drew an audible breath. "*You* sent that?"

Van shrugged. "It helps. So does being on deck, in the fresh air. You can fix your gaze on a set point—"

"Like all that water?"

Suppressing a smile, he widened his hand against her lower back. "Trust me on this. You'll feel much better up on top."

Trust him? After he'd pulled this *surprise, I'm coming with you* stunt? After he'd dropped that sly suggestion about her feeling better on top.

Okay, Susannah conceded, perhaps she'd only imagined that double meaning. When she met his eyes, she read nothing beyond mild impatience when he asked, "Upstairs or down?"

Either way she had his company. Downstairs, alone. Upstairs, with the laconic-looking captain, as well. "Up," she decided. If she was going to humiliate herself by upending her breakfast, it might as well be with a full audience.

Five minutes later, she was happy with her decision. Whether it was the medication, the open air in her face or her preoccupation with Donovan close at her side didn't matter. She tipped her head back and the speed of their progress across the water whipped her hair into a dozen wild streamers and lashed colour into her face. If she just concentrated on that swift progress instead of each wave-to-wave bump she might live through this.

"Enjoying yourself?"

"'Enjoy' might be pushing it," she admitted with a rueful grimace. Until her feet were back on solid ground, that was as near to a smile as she could manage.

"Come on. We've got the sun on our skin for the first time in days. Poseidon's blessed us with calm water and a hot yacht and nothing for miles and miles but open water. Look at this place. How could you not get a kick out of this?"

Susannah's hands tightened their grip on the railing. Eyes fixed dead ahead on the distant chunk of land she'd chosen as her point of reference, she refused to surrender to temptation. She would not sneak a sideways look to see if his face reflected the appealing mix of reverence and quiet pleasure that coloured his voice. It was enough that it curled through her, blurring the edges of her senses and melting the grip of her fear another degree.

"I'm going to sit down," she decided.

"Stay." His hand closed over hers on the rail, warm and solid and grounding. "We're almost there."

Sure, they'd been speeding across the bay at a great rate of knots but they couldn't be even a quarter of the way to Appleton. Then, as if to make a liar of her judgment, the cruiser's speed slackened and she realised that she'd lost focus on the anchoring chunk of land.

It rose from the water before them, the white posts of the jetty a stark contrast to the thick green scrub.

Charlotte Island. A beat of alarm pulsed through her as she slowly turned to meet Donovan's cleverly guarded eyes. "Why are we stopping here? What is this about?"

Six

What is this about?

"This," Van said in response to her question. He turned to face the tiny pocket of land sitting in the middle of Stranger's Bay.

Until now, he'd kept his focus on Susannah—no hardship there—but now his narrowed gaze shifted over the island and his chest tightened with a familiar frustration. Despite its significance, despite his previous visit, there was nothing familiar in the rocky shoreline or the gentle lap of waves against a bite of sand or the sharp roofline he could see peering out above the trees.

This time, he didn't even attempt to shuck the vise-like grip of emotion. He let it take hold, let it mould his mood as the yacht cruised in to the pier. A lone figure waited there, hand raised in greeting.

"The caretaker," Van said, turning back to Susannah. "Gilly's giving him a lift into town."

"We're just stopping to pick up another passenger?"

"And to let one off. I'm stopping here," he said. "For a couple of nights."

He watched her take that in, saw the slight easing of tension around her mouth. The infinitesimal slump of her shoulders. But when she pushed her sunglasses to the top of her head, the gaze she turned on his was clouded with confusion. "What did you mean by *this?*" she asked.

"This is why I want The Palisades. This is why that substitute property you offered to find for me was irrelevant."

"You want this island, not the resort?"

Lifting a hand from the rail, she grabbed her hair into that makeshift ponytail just as the yacht came to a rocky halt. She lost her balance for an instant, until Van steadied her with a hand at her elbow. She regained her foothold quickly, but he didn't let her go. "I take it you didn't come out here with me last time?"

"No."

"Because of your aversion to boats?"

"You didn't come by boat last time. You had the helicopter drop you off. And you didn't invite me," she added with a tight shrug that missed casual by at least a nautical mile. "I rather gathered that you wanted a break."

"From you? I rather doubt that."

Their gazes met and the inference of Van's rejoinder hummed between them. Wary heat flared in her eyes and low in Van's belly. He lifted a hand and threaded a loose strand of windswept hair behind her ear, and she shook her head slightly as if to refocus. "Why is the island so important?" she asked.

Van let his hand slide from her elbow to her hand. "Come and steady your legs on solid ground," he said, "and I'll tell you."

Feet fixed firmly on something that didn't rock and roll *and* an answer to the puzzle of why he wouldn't let The Palisades go. How could Susannah resist a double-edged invitation like that?

Once on firm land, she realised just how shaky her sea legs were, so when Donovan suggested they stroll down to the beach, she had no objection. After a short distance her legs started to feel more normal and so did her head. "This is why you came back," she mused.

She felt his glance on her face. "Here?"

"To Stranger's Bay. If you'd only wanted to apply pressure about the deal, you could have landed on my doorstep in Melbourne or gone straight to Alex."

"I needed to come back here. To see if I remembered."

Retracing his footsteps, recreating the past weekend. Last night's anxiety over that endeavour resurfaced in a slither of unease that travelled the length of Susannah's spine and tingled in the palm of her hand. Where he'd held it, she realised, last night and again leaving the boat just now.

It should have seemed small, insignificant, compared to all the intimacies they'd shared already. But it didn't. Perhaps because they'd skipped the preliminaries and landed straight in bed the first night, perhaps because he'd returned as a virtual stranger with no memory of those intimacies, perhaps because beyond the innocent touch she felt every memory in vivid, visceral detail.

She pushed both hands deep into the pockets of her trench coat and forced her focus back to his words. "You needed to come out here, to Charlotte Island, to see if you remembered that first visit?"

He didn't respond immediately, pausing instead to help her down a rocky section of path. They'd come quite a distance from the boat—far enough for her peace of mind. She glanced back to where it sat, rocking peacefully to sleep in the deep-blue water.

"You said I mentioned Mac."

Susannah's attention shifted back to his face, the boat instantly forgotten. "Only in passing, when I asked who the MacCreadie was in the Keane MacCreadie business name."

"Elaine MacCreadie," he supplied now. He started to move as he talked, and she kept pace beside him, her eyes trained on his face. "She was a client when I worked on Wall Street, a businesswoman with a boat-load of investments and a steel-trap brain. She said she appreciated my low BS quotient, and when I was shafted by one of the big bosses, she encouraged me to go it alone. She provided the start-up capital and the smart advice. I provided the man hours." He cut her a look. "Did I tell you she's an Aussie?"

"No, you didn't."

"From here," he said, indicating *right here* with a sweep on his hand. "Born and raised on Charlotte Island."

Susannah stopped dead in her tracks. "You're buying the place on her behalf."

"I'm buying it *for* her," he said, making the distinction with subtle emphasis as his eyes locked on hers. "Is there anyone in your life you would do anything for?"

"There was," she replied without hesitation. "My grandfather. Pappy Horton."

"Then you understand."

"I'm not sure that I do," she said slowly. "There is a wealth of difference between doing something and buying something."

"You think that's what I'm doing? Making an expensive gesture?" He expelled a rough breath and turned to stare fixedly out to sea for a long moment. And when he continued, there was a raw note to his voice she'd never heard before. A note that ripped straight to her heart. "Mac's not well. Hasn't been for a while now. This is probably my last chance to do something for her, and the one thing that would have any damn meaning would be seeing this place back in MacCreadie ownership."

"Does she have family?"

"A grandson."

And this would be her legacy to him, a link to his heritage in Australia.

"So, you understand why I won't give this up without a fight?" he asked.

"Mostly," Susannah said huskily, forcing the words past the thick ache at the back of her throat. "Although I don't understand why you didn't tell me about Mac before."

"It's not something I talk about," he said, and the shutters had come down on his eyes, just as they had done in the past when she'd asked anything too personal.

"Then why now?" she persisted, wanting to batter down the barriers. Wanting, God help her, a piece of the man inside.

"I had to do something. You were leaving."

She was achingly aware of his meaning. She was leaving, she was marrying another man, he would lose this last tenuous toehold on his quest to repay Mac. But her heart imagined another meaning in his words, in the quicksilver flame of his eyes.

"It will make no difference," she said. "I can't change what's been set in motion."

"You can. If you don't marry Carlisle." His gaze dropped to her lips. "Stay, Susannah. Convince me that this marriage is what you really want."

This is what she'd expected last night and she'd armed herself against the assault. Now he'd caught her unprepared. She needed to breathe, to ease the swell of emotion in her chest, to think. "I can't stay, Donovan. I can't."

"I'm afraid you have no choice."

"I don't know…" Her voice and her thoughts trailed off as she detected a new determination in his expression. She turned quickly, eyes drawn to the empty jetty and then to the gleam of white speeding away from the island.

"You brought me here, you talked me into leaving the boat and you'd already arranged for Gilly to leave without me?"

Van knew she wouldn't be happy. He was ready to face the heat of her anger, to answer all accusations, but the disenchantment burning at the back of her eyes caught him low and hard.

"Hey," he said softly. "I had reasons."

Giving in to the temptation to touch her, to soothe her, to hold her, he started forward, but she backed away as far as the water's edge, both hands raised with the same warning that flashed in her eyes.

"Last night I spent half the night worrying over why you'd left so easily. That was so out of character for a man who always pursues what he wants without compromise. Now I see. You were already planning this. You teased me about restraint and force and abduction—"

"Hang on just a second," he cut in.

But she wasn't hanging on for even half that time. She continued down that same path, her eyes growing more disillusioned with each word. "But you didn't have to resort to force, did you? Not when you could manipulate my emotions so easily. Sending me the seasick medication, your solicitous attention on the boat and then you crown it all with Mac. You know what? I would have preferred if you *had* brought me here by force. At least that would have been honest."

"You think I lied to you?"

"I think you manipulated me."

Van's eyes narrowed at that accusation. At the implication that he'd bent the truth, that he'd used Mac's illness in an underhanded way. "After the way you and your mother manipulated Carlisle on this deal, I'd be careful which stones you sling from that glass house, Susannah."

For a beat of time, that softly spoken counterstroke hung between them. Then she lifted her chin and he noted that the earlier swirl of disappointment had turned to cool disdain. "How long are you holding me hostage?" she asked.

"As long as it takes."

"To?"

"Stop you marrying Alex Carlisle."

Van's luggage, her one bag and the fresh food supplies sent over for their stay had all been delivered to the house perched high on the island's highest ridge. The original weatherboard cottage where Mac had spent her childhood was now the caretaker's residence. In recent years, the resort had added the luxurious timber lodge to its private island; the ultimate get-away-from-civilisation retreat with no phones, no television, no Internet.

"Ever been out here before?" Van asked, joining Susannah on the long veranda. The sweeping vista of water added to the sense of sitting in majestic isolation, alone in the middle of the wild and rugged southern ocean.

When she didn't answer his question, he let it slide. He figured she would get over her huff soon enough—possibly when he divulged why he'd sought her out. "I have a small favour to ask."

Her fingers curled around the railing, as if to consolidate her grip. "A favour?" She might as well have said, "A slimy toad?" She employed the same level of distaste.

"I'm heading out to take some photos," he told her.

"Have fun."

At least she was talking, Van decided. He much preferred these snooty comebacks to the frosty silence of their walk up from the beach. "It's not a sightseeing stroll. I want photos for Mac."

"You didn't think of that last time?" She favoured him with an incredulous look. "You had a camera with you the morning you came out here."

"Yeah, I had a camera. I had photos. Past tense."

Realisation flitted across her expression and her gaze snapped to his. "They stole your camera?"

He didn't answer. He just held her gaze a moment longer before asking again, "Will you help me out with the pictures?"

"Why do you need my help?"

"Mac wants a shot of me, at the cottage."

"I'll help," she said. "But just so you know, I'm doing it for Mac, not as a favour to you."

Van stretched the afternoon excursion for photos as far as he could, until the impatience simmering beneath her ice-cool facade snapped. He'd been helping her down a steep path at the time, his destination a stretch of virgin sand he'd glimpsed from the elevated veranda. But instead of giving him her hand, she slapped the digital camera into his outstretched palm.

"I think you have more than enough pictures of yourself," she said. "I'm not a mountain goat. I'm not dressed for hiking. I'm going back to take a shower."

Two hours later, Van knocked on the door of her bedroom—on arrival, he'd offered her the upstairs master, and after a suspicious moment's deliberation, she'd accepted. Now he gave her ample time to make herself decent or to tell him to go to hell, but beyond the door he heard nothing.

With her fear of boats, surely she wouldn't attempt to escape. Still, a tinge of worry clawed at his gut. He'd brought her here and he would keep her safe.

He knocked again, and when she didn't answer this time, he opened the door. Perhaps she was out on the balcony, out of earshot…

She wasn't.

Wrapped in a bath towel, she sat in the middle of the king-size bed, legs long and bare, hair a wet tangle of curls, her face turned toward the stunning view of tree-tops and ocean beyond the wall of louvred windows. Van paid scant attention to the backdrop. There was something in the picture she painted—not her unenhanced beauty, nor the knowledge of all that skin warm and scented from her shower, but the fragility of her expression—that stirred a world of yearning inside Van.

It echoed the moment down at the beach when she'd looked at him with naked disappointment; when he'd reached for her and she'd slapped him down. This time he forced himself not to reach. He sucked up that desire and waited a patient count of five for her to acknowledge his presence.

When she didn't, irritation ate away at his patience. "Still sulking?"

"Thinking, actually."

"About?"

"Our conversation down at the beach." She turned her head a fraction, enough that the angled rays of the sun caught her hair with fire. His breath caught with the same hot burn when he saw the hint of moisture on her lashes, the uneven redness in her cheeks.

She'd been crying.

"When you asked me if there was one person I would do anything for, I answered reflexively. There are others I'd also walk on hot coals for. Zara says I need to cultivate a little healthy selfishness. She thinks I'm a sap."

"Zara is your sister?" he guessed.

She nodded in silent assent. "She is also on my list of people I would do anything for, but Pappy came to mind instantly even though he's been gone ten years. Probably because I didn't have a chance to do any last things for him. He was gone too quickly." Her gaze lifted and locked on his. "She's dying, isn't she?"

The frankness of her question knocked the remaining air from Van's lungs. He couldn't answer. Ultimately he didn't have to because the sudden sheen of understanding in her eyes reflected his answer.

"That's what I thought." Lips pressed hard together, she turned away. "Did you only come up here to enquire about my sulking, or was there something else?"

"I brought you some clothes. I thought you might appreciate something clean to change into for dinner."

He put them down on the dresser beside the door, and prepared to leave before he said any more. Before he revealed the tenuous thread of emotion unravelling inside. He was halfway out the door when she spoke again.

"Mac's your grandmother, isn't she? You're the grandson."

Sucker punched by her perceptiveness, Van didn't answer. He didn't turn around. He kept on walking.

Seven

When the shadows of dusk fell over the house, Van started a fire in the huge open fireplace that dominated the living room. Susannah hadn't made an appearance—he didn't know if she would—and for a while after he'd come downstairs, he'd been glad. He'd needed time and solitude to soothe the raw emotion prodded to life by her perceptive questions.

That was done now, courtesy of the Vivaldi he'd set on rotation and the therapeutic benefit of applying a large knife to raw foodstuffs. The sauce for a simple pasta marinara now simmered on the stovetop. A bottle of light red breathed on the countertop. And he'd reminded himself of what mattered.

Not filling his memory with details of Susannah Horton, not wiping disenchantment or tears from her eyes, not protecting his male pride from further bruising.

If Susannah joined him for dinner, he would use whatever compassion he'd stirred up with today's revelations to pursue his goal. If she didn't come downstairs, then there was always the option of delivering room service. This time he'd be better prepared. He wouldn't let the sight of her naked vulnerability put him on the back foot; he would use it to his own advantage.

As much as he enjoyed the notion of feeding her by the fireside, the image of her stretched out on that bed, dressed in the clothes he'd left...*his* clothes, against *her* skin...lit a different kind of fire. When he caught the first shadow of movement on the stairs, he suffered a minor jab of letdown. The bedroom alternative had been looking so very attractive.

He closed the pantry door, the linguine he'd been searching out in hand, and the sight of her coming down the stairs incinerated the disappointment and redefined his definition of attractive.

He'd wondered how she would take to the intimacy of wearing his clothes...especially the boxer shorts. But, no. There they were, peeping out from beneath the hem of his 49ers sweatshirt. It hung halfway to her knees but still exposed enough of her long, slender legs to turn his mouth dry.

Two stairs from the bottom, she caught him eyeing those legs and stopped dead in her tracks. Palpable tension crackled in the air between them until Van forced his gaze away. If this was going to work—if he was going to build her sympathy into seduction—then he needed to make her comfortable. Keeping his eyes above her collarbone would be a good start.

Depositing the forgotten pasta on the countertop, he nodded at the outfit. "Nice look."

Still looking wary, she descended the last couple of stairs. "I appreciated having something clean to put on. Thank you."

"I have my moments."

"This was a good one," she conceded. Across the width of the living room their eyes met and held, the caution in hers edged with her gratitude. A promising start, Van decided. But then she straightened her shoulders and started toward the kitchen like a woman on a mission. "I'm just going to grab something to eat in my room."

"No need to do that. Dinner's coming along. Why don't you sit by the fire? There's antipasto to tide you over. Wine, beer, soda—take your pick."

She hesitated, her nostrils flaring slightly as if taking in the flavoursome aromas wafting from the kitchen.

"Linguine Marinara. My signature dish."

"You cooked?" she asked on a note of surprise. "From scratch?"

"No need to sound so stupefied."

"In July, you told me you travelled too much to bother keeping a home. You ate out. You ordered in. So, yes, I am surprised that your culinary skills have progressed from microwave reheating to claiming a signature dish."

"There has to be an upside to being off work for weeks on end."

Her wary gaze turned serious as she met his eyes. "It's nice that you could take a positive from that experience."

"Learning my way around the kitchen was one," he supplied with a half-shrug. "Why don't you take a seat? Your waiter will be along shortly."

She hesitated, but only briefly, before crossing to the fireside. In that moment's pause, Van saw the questions in her eyes, and while he watched her sit on a cushion beside the hearth, he staunched his instinctive resistance.

He'd snared her curiosity. She would stay. They would talk. He would soothe the remaining apprehension from her eyes, the same as he'd done last night.

Except this time, he wasn't leaving.

"Wine?"

"Thank you, yes." Twisting at the waist, she looked back at him over her shoulder. The curiosity he'd detected earlier came alive in her face as she watched him pour and then transfer the appetisers to a serving plate. "Is waiting tables another skill you picked up while you were in stasis…or would that have been superfluous?"

"I live alone, if that's what you're asking."

"I thought, given your circumstances…"

"That I might have needed live-in assistance?"

She shuffled her position on the cushion, presumably so she wouldn't crick her waist or neck looking back at him. The new position afforded him an excellent view of her killer legs, but that was a momentary distraction. Her next comment brought all his attention winging back to her face. "Actually, I wondered if you may have moved in with Mac. She is your only family, right?"

Ever since she'd asked the question upstairs, he'd

known she would return to his relationship with Mac. He hadn't expected the edge to her tone, however. Hands planted on the bench, he held her chary gaze. "Why do I sense that you won't believe my answer?"

"In July you said you had no family. I believed that."

"In July I had no family."

"And now you suddenly do?"

"Another of those upsides I mentioned."

She shook her head slowly, her expression a mix of confusion and exasperation. "You acquired a grandmother?"

That pretty much summed it up. And if he concentrated on the upside instead of the hot cauldron of regret and frustration that seethed inside him then he could impart the bare facts. "Mac had an unplanned pregnancy when she was a teenager, a daughter she gave up for adoption. She didn't track her down until ten years ago. By then my mother was long dead."

"But she found you?"

"She sought me out, became my client. She never intended to tell me about our relationship."

"Whyever not?" A wealth of emotion swirled in her eyes as she looked up at him; the kind he'd sworn to avoid. The kind that stirred the hot ache in his gut. "Why did she bother finding you if she didn't want to claim you as her family?"

"She wanted to know me, to help me, but she could see I was doing fine without family."

"Then why tell you now?" she persisted. Half a second later, she made a rough sound of discovery and distress. "I answered that earlier, upstairs, didn't I?"

"Yes, she's dying." He shrugged, a tight gesture that

did nothing to ease the tension in his muscles. "But that wasn't the only motivation. When I woke up in hospital with this amnesia, she talked to help me work out what I remembered and what I didn't. Then when I was recovering, we just talked, a lot. Not only about business or politics or the state of the economy. She told me about her past. Her regrets. When she started talking about my mother, the rest came out."

"That must have been quite a shock."

He brought her glass of wine and hunkered down to put it in her hand. Then he took his own seat on the floor, close enough that their knees brushed with a frisson of heat. It was a response he welcomed, the physical that he understood and could deal with, that didn't burn like twisted metal in his gut. "Don't feel sorry for me, Susannah. As you so accurately put it, I acquired myself a grandmother."

"A grandmother you're going to lose," she said, and the emotion in her eyes—and his body's response— blew away the remnant heat of the physical contact. When he would have pulled away from that confronting emotion, she leaned forward and captured him with the quiet intensity of her gaze. "I know you said I couldn't understand what you've been through but some of this I do know."

"Your grandfather?"

She nodded. "He loved to fish. That was his escape from the pressure of corporate life and the pretensions of society. He hated the functions he was forced to attend…he despised small talk. One weekend he went out chasing the big fish and he didn't come home."

"Hence your aversion to boats?" he guessed.

"No, that's all about the seasickness. Although I suspect psychologists would have a field day with the connection." A whisper of a smile touched her lips. "Pappy Horton was…he was so much more than the tycoon robber-baron the media depicted."

"I'm sorry."

"So was I. He left me his cabin in the high country where we stayed when he took me trout fishing."

Her wistful expression stirred an unfamiliar emotion in Van's gut. Part was the dull ache of empathy, part the sharper need to stop her hurt, to turn the storm clouds gathering in her eyes to smiles. "You fish? If you think I'll buy that—" he shook his head, exaggerating his surprise "—how big was the one that got away?"

"My grandfather taught me how to fly cast when I was knee-high to a grasshopper."

Eyebrows raised, Van studied her in this new light. Even dressed as she was in his oversize clothes, Susannah exuded class and city style. He couldn't for the life of him picture her in the guise of fisherwoman. "I am impressed."

"Not half as much as when I caught the first bream from the rocks!"

A reference to their last weekend—to a happening Van didn't remember. He could have pursued that angle; he could have sought more detail; he could have teased her about the relative merits of their catches.

But as he watched the play of firelight in her hair and the play of shadows in her eyes, the past held no interest. He wanted to know her, not to engage his memory, not to kill the sale contract on The Palisades, but for himself, for this moment of time.

"This cabin," he began. "Do you go there often?"

"I always seem to be too busy." She shook her head and made a rueful sound. "And that's no excuse. I did take Zara once. I taught her the grand tradition of the Pappy Horton fly cast. She was a natural."

"Your grandfather didn't teach her?"

"He never met Zara. She's my half sister, you see." The smile brimming in her eyes clouded with regret. "We only found out about each other a few years back when she came searching for her father."

"And she found you?"

"Fortunately, yes."

Her gaze fell away, lost in silent introspection of her untouched wine. Forgotten along with the plate of appetisers. Van wanted to continue feeding a different appetite, reconstructing his image of the woman inside the polished facade. The woman who looked more comfortable in a sweatshirt and bare feet than in a buttoned-up designer coat.

"Is your sister like you?" he asked.

She took a slow sip from her wine, her eyes meeting his over the rim of her glass before she lowered it. Something had shifted in the mood, he realised, in the last minute or two. The earlier conflict and mistrust soothed by a new understanding and empathy. "You asked that same question the first time I told you about my family."

"And how did you answer?"

"I said, not at all. Zara is a knockout. Tall, blond,

beautiful. She's studying medicine, so she's super smart and dedicated to a future in medical research. And as if that's not enough, she's also athletic and works part-time as a personal trainer. If I didn't love her, I might possibly hate her for all that amazingness!"

Van smiled at her deprecating tone. "I imagine you're more alike than you credit."

"And *that's* also the same response as last time."

"Are you suggesting I'm predictable? Unoriginal? Boring?"

She laughed, a soft, husky chuckle that drew his gaze back to her lips. To the pinkened sheen left by the wine. To the satisfaction of knowing that the vibe arcing between them was here and now and only about them. "Oh, no," she said softly. "You are many things and not one of them boring."

In the aftermath of that admission their gazes tangled in a ripple of sensual energy, as delicate and multifaceted and intoxicating as the pinot noir she lifted to her lips. He could have asked about those many nonboring things, but only one held his focus.

"Was it like this before?" He gestured between them, illustrating the subtle tension that he couldn't label with words.

"Yes. Always."

The honesty in her answer was real. No question, no hesitation, no artifice. And whether she realised that she'd been too candid or whether she saw the intent in his eyes—whatever the reason, her expression grew cautious as Van removed the glass from her hand and, eyes locked on hers, set it down on the hearth tiles.

The wary widening of her eyes sparked a surge of satisfaction deep in his chest. The heat of contact as he rested his hand on her knee sparked something more primitive lower in his body.

He leaned closer and she drew a swift breath. "No. Don't."

But that was all the objection he allowed her. He didn't want the spectre of her arranged marriage hovering between them, didn't want the name of her sainted fiancé on her tongue.

He took her chin in his hand and silenced any complaint with his lips on hers. Beneath his touch she stiffened in surprise or in denial, and his objective instantly changed shape. No longer intent on simply tasting, he wanted her response, her acceptance, her participation.

Her kiss.

Cradling her face between his hands, he gentled the initial pressure of his mouth on hers. He traced the shape of her lips, kissed the corners and the dip in her chin, held her captive in the snare of his gaze before he reclaimed her mouth in a long, slow seduction. For a while he lost himself and the passage of time as he learned her taste and the silky texture of her skin beneath his hands.

Her hands, lifted initially to push him away, clutched in his shirtfront and the sound against his lips was a throaty mix of satisfaction and surrender. That evocative sound and the first stroke of her tongue against his fired something in Van's synapses. A burst of vivid memory of her giving mouth under his, his hands twined in her hair as he rolled her beneath him, the sun streaming through glass to set fire to her red-gold hair and to the passion drumming through his blood. And the echo of his voice deep in his mind.

Now I have you right where I want you.

He ended the kiss abruptly, shocking Susannah up from the sensual depths with the lash of an earthy curse. She stared up at him, clueless as to its motivation. One second he'd been immersed in the kiss, in her mouth, in sliding his free hand from knee to thigh; the next, abandonment.

"What's going on?" she asked slowly. "What just happened there?"

"I thought I—" He broke off, raked a hand through his hair, let go his breath in a sharp exhalation. And when he started to turn away, Susannah grabbed at his sleeve and forced his attention back to her. "For a moment—not even a second—I had this...flash."

"You remembered?"

"I don't know. I don't even know that it was an accurate memory or a..." He lifted a shoulder and let it drop, but the enormity of his frustration resonated in the deepened rasp of his voice. "I don't know what I recognised. It was just an impression of you and a line of dialogue."

"I didn't say anything. I couldn't." Apart from the fact of her tongue being elseways occupied, the overwhelming impact of his kiss had stolen her ability to think in whole words. "Was it something you remembered me saying?"

"No, not you, *me.* And I don't know if it's something

I said to you. It was there in my mind, as clear as if a light had switched on, and then gone—" he clicked thumb against finger "—like that. I'm left with one pinpoint of illumination in a big, dark void and I don't know if it's a memory or a figment of fantasy."

A reflection of that fantasy flared in his eyes for a moment, alerting Susannah to its erotic nature. She relinquished her grip on his sleeve. She didn't want to pursue this. She wanted to spring to her feet and run, hard and fast, from everything this man aroused in her— the physical, the emotional, the then and the now.

The knowledge that she could never have him; that she could never tell him what they had shared for such a fleetingly fragile piece of time.

But the storm of frustration raging in his eyes— not sexual frustration, but the exasperation of not remembering—plumbed the depths of her heart. How could she turn her back? How could she not try to help?

"It may well have been a memory," she commenced cautiously. Nervous fingers, the same ones that had gripped his shirt and held his mouth hard against hers, curled into the cushion beneath her backside. She tightened her thighs, tucking her knees closer beneath her in a vain attempt to quash the heat he'd ignited in her body. "Do you want to tell me about that line of dialogue?"

He stared back at her for a long second, the frustration honed to razor's-edge sharpness. "Just tell me one thing. Did I make any promises to you?"

Susannah's heart thumped heavily against her ribs. She couldn't tell him. Opening up that wound in her heart would serve no purpose.

Mustering every ounce of bravado, she met his eyes and for the first time in her life, she straight-out lied to him. "There were no promises, Donovan. None whatsoever."

Van didn't believe her but he curbed the desire to call her on the lie. Pushing to establish the truth about past promises would put her on the defensive again. Right now he needed—and wanted—to concentrate on the present and keeping her in the same room, in his company, was tantamount to his plans.

Putting a stop to her marriage, he realised, had become more than a means to securing a deal. Through dinner he watched her eat, drink, talk, and all he could think about was that mouth beneath his. Not as a conduit to the past, but because he wanted. For him, for now.

The craving coiled more tightly with each passing minute, every awkward pause, each time her gaze slipped away from his. And with each passing minute the certainty grew that she, too, was steeped in the same sweet agony of wanting. It was in the heightened colour that traced her cheekbones, the unsettled play of her fingers against glass and tableware, the falsely cheerful bursts of small talk that grew less frequent and more desultory as the meal stretched on.

Van could have picked up the conversational reins, but some perverse part of him enjoyed the crackle of tension in the lengthening silences. He let it play out as long as he could, until she set down her napkin and started packing up the plates. "Leave them," he said. And when she looked like protesting, "The dishes aren't going anywhere and neither are we. They'll still be there in the morning."

"And so will we," she said, and the spark in her voice was reflected in her eyes as they met his. This time they didn't drift away. "For how many more mornings?"

"Why don't we take this conversation to the fireside," Van suggested smoothly. "I'll make coffee."

"No, thank you."

"Okay, so no coffee."

"And no fireside conversation," she added. "Please, Donovan, just answer my question. When is Gilly returning to pick us up?"

"When our business here is finished."

"Our business?" She leaned forward in her chair, her fingers tight on the plates she'd yet to relinquish. "How can we even start to sort out this mess when we're stuck here?"

"That's not the only business. *We* have unfinished business."

For a moment his words hung between them, and Van felt a kick of anticipation when their meaning registered in her expressive eyes. They darkened to a turbulent sea-green as she shook her head.

"You're denying there's something between us? After that kiss?" Van's voice deepened with the memory, with the impact, with the certainty that he would have that mouth under his again. "I can still feel it, Susannah. I can still taste you in my blood."

"That doesn't change anything."

"Doesn't it? What if I hadn't stopped? What if that kiss had continued the way it started? What if you'd ended up naked with me inside you?"

"Then I would know that you'd succeeded," she replied. "You brought me here for one reason. You want to end my marriage plans—what better way than by seducing me?"

"It's not only about the deal, Susannah. You're discounting this burn between us."

"I'm not discounting it. How can I?" she asked simply, but the heat of passion was in her eyes, in her cheeks, in the throaty ache of her voice. "But as much as I want you, Donovan Keane, there is one thing I'm determined not to do. My father cheated, with Zara's mother and Lord knows how many other women, and he hurt a lot of people in the process.

"I would never do that to Alex," she continued in the same softly impassioned tone. "I would never do that to anyone I respected, and I don't believe you would want me to. Not even to win this deal for Mac."

Eight

Van had no argument and no countermeasure. If he forced the issue, he would lose her respect and sometime during the past twenty-four hours that had assumed a vital importance.

Yet everything inside him rebelled against standing aside. For close to two months he'd been forced to do nothing. Impatience, impotence, thwarted desire—hell, there must have been a dozen other equally abhorrent ingredients curdling in his gut. A long night where his insomnia kicked in—and where he'd heard Susannah moving restlessly upstairs into the early hours—had done nothing to improve his outlook.

Neither did the storm clouds darkening the southern sky.

They'd come up quickly in the late morning, as if

summoned by his own turbulent mood. He'd tried to run that from his blood in a controlled set of sprints up and down the sandy curve of beach. It had worked for the time he'd taken climbing the steep incline back to the house.

Lost in contemplation of the lunch he aimed to prepare after a long, relaxing shower, he started shucking his sweat-dampened shirt as he came in the door. Susannah sat curled up on a sofa. A book lay open on her lap but her gaze was fixed on those billowing clouds until his arrival startled it back toward the door.

Then she focussed on his bare chest and Van's post-exercise relaxation evaporated under her silent scrutiny.

When her sea-green concern shifted to his face, she must have read the warning signs in his hardened expression. Smart woman; she didn't say a word about the scars, but as he crossed to his bedroom he felt the incendiary touch of those eyes track his every step.

"Is Gilly coming today?" she asked.

"No." And he felt mean and moody enough to pause with his hand on the door to add, "If you're concerned about this weather coming in, there's a small runabout in the boatshed. We can leave now."

"How small?"

He turned back. Her fingers had quite a grip on the book; but she still held her chin high and proud. Despite her fear, she was actually considering this option, and while he showered, he recalled a snatch of conversation from the previous evening. When she'd told him about her grandfather who'd gone out fishing and never come back.

* * *

He came out of his room fifteen minutes later with an apology ready, but she was gone. From the veranda he caught sight of her down by the boathouse—checking the size of the runabout?—and he cursed himself for mentioning it.

Two hours later, she still hadn't returned. The concern gnawing away inside took a stronger bite. Surely she wouldn't do something so stupid. She didn't only dislike boats, they straight-out petrified her.

Then he saw movement on the track just above the pier. The white of his shirt—this morning he'd left it and a pair of his trackpants outside her door—as she loped into view. Not dawdling, but not exactly making haste.

His chest tightened with a contradictory mix of intense relief and annoyance.

If she didn't get a wriggle on, she'd be caught out in the storm. Right on cue, the clouds growled ominously and the first fat drops fell from the darkening sky. Van hit the steps at a run.

He found her a couple of minutes down the track, just as the heavens opened. By the time they made it back to the house they were both drenched and Van itched for a confrontation. The island's terrain was barely friendly at the best of times. In the rain she could have lost her way, slipped, fell.

Beneath the shelter of the porch, he rounded on her. "Have you no sense of self-preservation?"

Gathering her wet hair in hand, she paused. Her eyes met his and held. "I thought I did. I didn't take the boat."

Hell. She had considered it.

Fear, cold and fierce, held him in its talons for several rough heartbeats. And when he caught up with her at the door he saw that she wasn't only wet, she was shivering cold. He pushed the door open and, when she didn't move, urged her forward with a firm hand at her back.

"You're freezing." Shouldering the door shut behind her, he indicated the unused bedroom with a curt nod. "That shower's closest. Go warm yourself under it. I'll get you dry clothes."

"I'll use—"

"Don't argue, or I'll pick you up and carry you in there myself."

When her mouth tightened mulishly, Van took an advancing step. She took several backward, her hands held up in a stay-right-there gesture. They were trembling with cold.

"I'm going. I can manage."

Van wasn't so sure. Eyes narrowed, he watched her retreat. Despite the trembling hands she started to unbutton the shirt as she walked. "Are you able to manage the buttons?"

In the doorway she half turned, and he noticed what he'd been too fractious to notice before. The rain had soaked right through, and the shirt clung to her skin revealing the lines of her lacy bra and the lush shape of her breasts. His thighs tightened with a jolt of desire so strong it riveted him to the spot.

An image flashed through his brain and his blood, his hands unthreading buttons, the shadow of aureole through sheer lace, the kiss of her silken skin beneath his tongue.

Slowly, finally, he lifted his gaze. Their eyes clashed with heated knowledge but she didn't bolt or berate him. She faced him with pride and poise and answered the question he'd long since forgotten asking. "I can manage."

Susannah spent only enough time in the shower to warm herself through. She couldn't afford to loiter, to allow her mind to linger over the way he'd looked at her and the way she'd looked back. She wouldn't think about him soaked to the skin, the fine white fabric plastered against hard muscles…or peeled off.

No. She would not think about Donovan Keane undressing. She. Would. Not.

She wrenched the shower controls off but the muted sound of running water continued, filling her senses with a crystal clear image of tall, dark and naked. Right next door. The knowledge that he was warming his chilled body the other side of this thin wall stripped her of all discipline for several steamy seconds.

Then she grabbed a towel, intent on racing upstairs and locking her unruly self away until the storm had passed—or at least the tumult in her body—but in the bedroom she pulled up short. Laid out on the bed was another set of clean clothes, chosen by him, for her use. There was no other explanation for their presence in this unused room.

Quickly she gathered them up and with an ear to the next room—shower still running, time to make good her escape—she made a dash for the stairs and didn't stop until she was leaning her back against the closed and secured door. Her breath was coming hard, and not only from the mad sprint. The soft cotton fabric of the under-shirt and snug white boxers clutched to her breast seemed incredibly intimate.

Yes, they were clean but he'd worn them at some point. Against his bare skin. If she had any sense of self-preservation, she would discard them in favour of her own underwear, washed and drying over the towel rail in her bathroom.

If she had any sense of self-preservation, she would drop all the damn clothes and kick them to kingdom come. She would remind herself how he'd trapped her here against her will, a virtual prisoner, and that he had no right to redress her for being caught out in the rain. She should be a dozen kinds of riled with him, but how could she when she understood his motivation?

Is there a person in your life you would do anything for?

Last night he'd vacillated over her appeal for respect, but in the end, he'd let her go.

Today he'd come out in the rain looking for her, making sure she made it back to the house safely.

Then he left the clothes.

Every one of those factors, she realised with a gloomy sense of fatalism, spelled more danger to her self-resolve than a hundred imaginings of wet, well-toned muscles.

A renewed squall of rain-heavy wind blasted her windows and shuddered through the house, a timely reminder of the storm's growing ferocity. She pushed off the door and dressed quickly. In her own clothes. And despite her earlier vows to seclude herself up here, she knew the howling insistence of that wind would drive her down to the security and the warmth of the lower level.

Why delay the inevitable?

Downstairs she could find something to occupy her mind...or at least redirect her thoughts. Although the resort promoted a get-away-from-the-modern-world ethos, they supplied indoor entertainment in the form of an extensive library of books and music and old-fashioned board games.

Who are you kidding? Downstairs there is Donovan, the only entertainment needed to fully occupy your mind.

Her stomach tightened with nervous apprehension as she descended the stairs. She hadn't wasted a lot of time dressing; she'd given up on pretending to tame her hair days ago, securing it in a loose braid. And, okay, she still had enough vanity remaining to apply tinted moisturiser but that was it.

Yet, he'd beaten her to the living room. Squatting down at the fireplace, he applied match to kindling and the fire caught in a crackle and hiss of sparks. The same sensation roared through Susannah's senses when the flames limned his profile in golden light.

What was it about this man, his particular masculine beauty? Why him, why this connection, this depth of knowing and wanting?

Then he turned, saw her and unwound his sinuously muscled frame to its full six and a bit feet of familiar impact. Outside the storm howled a warning to bunker down, take cover, stay safe; inside her mind a voice cried the same warning. It went unheeded, drubbed out by the thundering of her heart.

"You're back to your own clothes," he said, taking in

her skirt and sweater. Stockings. Boots. "I hope you're comfortable."

"Not really," she admitted. After last night, that kiss, her response, there seemed little point in denying what simmered between them. "But your things—thank you, again. If this keeps up, I may need them tomorrow."

Reflexively, she lifted her hands to hug her upper arms.

Donovan's expression narrowed. "Are you cold? Come and sit by the—"

"No, not cold," she reassured him quickly. "It's the storm. The wind. I'm not a big fan of the rattling of glass."

"Bad experience?"

She nodded. "One of those trips to my grandfather's mountain cabin. And it is only a cabin, one room and outside bathroom. A real rustic retreat with no mod cons. It was Pappy's way of staying attuned to his roots."

"A self-made man?"

"Yes." Abandoning her sanctuary at the foot of the stairs, she came farther into the room. "Property, development, investments. Anyway, we were at the cabin one weekend and a storm came up and the whole place groaned and shook and this great big mountain gum came crashing down right at the edge of the porch. I didn't think I would live to see my ninth birthday."

"That would have been a pity," he said gravely. "I imagine birthdays in the Horton household would have been quite something."

"Oh, yes. Big showy somethings." She'd aimed for blithe, but somehow it came out sounding too cynical. Too revealing, under his silent regard. She expelled a

deprecating laugh. "As you can see, I survived un-
scathed. I suspect the storm wasn't as bad in reality as
in my imagination. Probably a tepid sea breeze compared to this. Upstairs, with the wall of windows—I
thought half the island might end up in my room."

As if to illustrate her point, the wind and rain buffeted
the eastern wall in a muscle-flexing show of strength. *I
am nature, hear me roar.* Susannah flinched, but Donovan
stood tall and unmoved. "This not-so-rustic retreat has
been built to withstand worse than this, Susannah."

"If you say so."

"I know so. I might not remember coming here, but
I had all the reports and appraisals. I knew exactly what
I was buying." His gaze, steady, strong, reassuring,
locked on hers. "You're safe here."

"Am I?"

There was a beat of pause, while the barely audible syl-
lables hummed between them. Last night, she'd asked the
question, he'd responded by walking away. Tonight,
before she settled, before she trusted, she needed his word.
"I brought you here, Susannah. I will keep you safe."

Susannah trusted him. The notion, surprising, pleasing,
terrifying, shifted the mood between them as the afternoon wore on. She refused to sit idly by the fire and be
waited on; he was no good at sitting and passing the time.

He hadn't needed to tell her that; it was part of his
will-do nature and part of the restless spirit that kept him
moving and seeking new challenges in business. Another reason why he had no need of a home.

She slotted another piece into the jigsaw puzzle

she'd been working on for the past half hour, before turning to track his progress into the kitchen. "Nuh-uh," she said with mild rebuke. "My turn to make dinner tonight."

"You cook?"

"Quite well, as it happens."

He leaned his hips against the island counter, folded his arms across his chest and a small grin tilted his mouth. "You don't say."

"What is the smile for?" she asked, suspicious.

"You."

Their eyes met in the wake of that simple response, but there was nothing simple about it. Asking for more was pure masochism but she couldn't stop herself. "Me…in what way?"

"You're a constant surprise. When I first saw you— even before I saw you—I pegged you as a princess."

"In wading boots and a tiara?"

The smile widened on his lips; deepened in her heart. "Now, there's a picture."

"I've always been more comfortable in the wading boots," she admitted, exaggerating a tony accent. "The tiara tends to get tangled in the hair."

"There is a lot to tangle in." His gaze tracked the braid and its many escaped strands, before returning to her face. "Is the colour natural?"

He'd asked that before. Their first night. Before he'd chosen to discover the truth in his own will-do fashion.

Her skin prickled with remembered heat, with the sensation of his fingers sliding beneath her skirt and stroking her inner thigh. And, damn her redhead's complexion, that memory suffused her skin with warmth and she swore he saw right through her discomfort to the very, very bad images playing in her mind.

"Yes," she said in a husky breath. "All natural."

The focus of his heavy-lidded eyes grew hazy as he considered her comment. "And the curls?"

"What you see is all me."

"Unaided and unabetted," he murmured, and the appreciation in his silky, low voice and the hooded heat of his gaze turned every nerve alive in Susannah's body. "Very unprincessy."

"That isn't entirely by choice. This—" she flipped the plait back over her shoulder "—would normally be blow-dried and straightened. There would be makeup. Zara maintains that I could groom and primp for Australia."

"You don't need to."

"Oh, yes. A princess who grows up with frizzy red hair and gangly legs and freckles, learns how to primp!"

He chuckled, a low, smoky sound that hummed through her heightened senses. It struck her that for all the time she'd spent with him that previous weekend and in the past few days, this was the first time she'd heard that devilish laugh. She'd barely had time to savour the new knowledge, to stow it away with all the other memories, before he said, "You grew up just fine, Princess."

They ended up preparing dinner together, a long and leisurely process drawn out by the mood of teasing truce they'd established. She told him she preferred Princess to Goldilocks. He chipped a place even deeper in her heart by asking what her Pappy had called her.

"Princess," she admitted. Then, to ease the sudden choking tension, she added with faux gravity, "Or by my full title, Princess Susannah of Horton Ponds."

"That works with the wading boots and fishing pole image."

"Exactly."

They returned to the business of dinner, working alongside each other in a delicious combination of accord and teasing dispute. They debated the optimum combination of herbs for the oven-baked schnapper, swapped tastes of fresh salad ingredients as they chopped and sliced, fought for control of the garlic press but not for the job of dicing onions.

But beneath the surface lurked the sleeping beast of their attraction, just waiting for the chance to pull them under.

Like when Susannah refused his offer of wine— "After last night…no, I'll refrain." And the memory of their kiss burned bright in his eyes.

Or when her hair came free of the braid while she was whisking the makings of a crème brûlée, and he stepped in and said, "Let me fix it for you." His voice, low and gruff, stroked her like roughened velvet and then his hands were in her hair rethreading the sections and filling her with a yearning for more. Then he stopped and she looked up and caught the flare of his nostrils and felt the glancing touch of his gaze on her erect nipples.

She could feel her body listing toward him, the pull so intense, so necessary, that she couldn't right herself.

Until a piercing crack of breaking timber shattered

the moment. Susannah yelped. The bowl clattered to the countertop. And Donovan was already halfway to the door, gone a second later.

A branch had come down on the front path. No damage to the house and a saving grace as far as Van was concerned. If Susannah had continued to look at him in that touch-me, take-me way, if she'd put that outstretched hand on him—anywhere—he would not have been accountable for his actions. It had taken a good ten minutes pacing around in the sleety wind to cool his body's raging need before he could trust himself to return indoors.

Two hours later, they had eaten, the storm had abated, but not before a second severed branch crashed noisily against the side of the house.

"I see what you meant by the scream," Van said, recalling the night at The Palisades when she'd threatened to scream the place down. Not a smart move, remembering, because with that recollection came the scent of her skin in his nostrils, the heat of her temper bubbling so close to the surface, the rising urge to get that close again.

"*That* wasn't a scream," she said now. "It was more of a…loud gasp."

Van leaned back in his chair and regarded her with a simmering mix of amusement and desire. Princess Susannah really was something. With every hour in her company there was something else. "Out of curiosity—what led to your hair-raising scream that other weekend?"

She, God help him, finished licking the caramelised sugar from her dessert spoon before answering. "A frog."

"Like Kermit?"

"An ugly frog. It may have been a toad," she added defensively. "We were in the hot tub and I turned to get something and it was sitting on the edge of the tub. Right. There."

"Don't princesses kiss frogs?"

"Princesses kiss princes."

He should have laughed. Or continued teasing her about the frog/toad. But somewhere in the midst of that exchange he got lost in the remembered taste of her kiss and the frustration he'd kept at bay bubbled to the surface. "Like Carlisle?" he asked.

The spoon went still in her fingers for a beat before she answered. "I've never kissed Alex."

Van's heartbeat seemed to slow and deepen with the magnitude of that admission. She'd never slept with Carlisle.

"Are you still going to marry him?"

"I don't know," she said. "I may have no alternative."

His eyes narrowed to silver-sharp slits. "Is that what you're looking for, Susannah. An alternative? In what form—another proposal?"

"No!" Chin up, she stared him down with what looked like genuine outrage. "I know that you don't want marriage. That you value your independence too much to be looking for permanent ties."

"Then what do you want? Would you like me to take the choice out of your hands? To get out of my chair and come around the table, pick you up and carry you into my bed and do—"

"No!"

"No, you don't want me?" His voice dropped, low and rough as his mood. "Liar."

"You know I want you," she fired back, an agony of that wanting in the vibrato edge to her voice. "And you know why I won't let myself have you."

"Your father, the cheat?"

"Yes. My father, the cheating bastard. I won't be him. And I won't go back on my word to Alex."

Heart in mouth, Susannah watched him rise to his feet. Would he come around the table? Would he force this issue, now, after ceding to her appeal last night? But all he said was, "I'm going to check if there's any damage outside."

"Can I help?"

Something like grim amusement ghosted over his face. "You can help by taking yourself to bed. Use the spare bedroom downstairs, if that makes you feel safer."

Her gaze flickered from the spare room to his, next door.

"Yeah." There was a wealth of meaning in that soft sound and the speculation that flared in his eyes caused her nipples to tighten into hard buds. "You might consider locking the door."

After he was gone she did consider the downstairs room, but then she recalled the adjoining showers and how vulnerable—and how tempted—she'd felt with only that one thin wall between them. All night, too near, too dangerous.

She could sleep upstairs. It was only wind. Yesterday she'd conquered a boat ride without humiliation. If she embraced this tumultuous night, who knew, tomorrow she might face down a frog.

She attacked the stairs and started undressing as soon as she closed the door. If she kept moving, without thinking, she could dive under the covers and stay there covered and secure. In the privacy of the bathroom she stripped out of her underwear and pulled on her makeshift nightdress.

Donovan's shirt.

The fabric shimmered against her oversensitised skin, as fine and cool as silk. Fitting for Princess Susannah. A small smile teased her lips as she folded back the cuffs and started buttoning.

Two buttons down a huge wrenching crash of wood against glass halted her fingers, and in the space of a heartbeat her smile turned to a scream.

Nine

The storm had passed, the night turned quiet but for the creaking of wet timber and the trickle of overflow from rooftop to ground. Van circled the house with a restless frustration. He should have rejoiced in the aftermath and the lack of damage to what could soon be his property, but the storm was still building to a thunderhead in his body.

He'd sent Susannah to bed, but a perverse part of him hoped she'd thumbed her nose at that edict. That he'd walk inside and find her curled up on the sofa, the fire-light painting golden shadows over her all-natural body. If that happened, then damn the trust she'd placed in him.

He paused beneath the window of the spare bedroom, dark, silent. Perhaps she had stayed up. His heartbeat quickened as he moved on, his steps surer and growing with purpose.

From the east side of the house he heard the wrenching crack of a limb breaking from a tree. The shuddering impact as it struck. But it was her scream, loud enough to split the night and his inflamed body asunder, that sent him careening into the house…only to find the spare bedroom empty. All of downstairs rooms were empty.

Wild with dread, he tackled the stairs three at a time, the pull of fear more powerful than the pull of pain in his tight hamstrings. He tore the door open and came to a brickwall halt when he saw the branch protruding through the shattered wall of windows. Sharp-ended timber and glass fragments littered the floor and bed, which was blessedly empty.

"Susannah!"

Her name rasped raw in his throat. Maybe he'd missed her downstairs. Maybe she'd been in his room, in his—

The bathroom door opened, the light illuminating the scene of destruction. Van heard her gasp, saw the shock on her blanched face as he barked an order to, "Stay put. Don't move."

She was in the bathroom, out of harm's way.

Van's brain deciphered the information but the fierce tension in his gut did not relent. The brittle crunch of glass beneath his feet twisted it tighter still as he crossed the room.

Without hesitation, he slid one arm under her thighs and the other around her back and picked her up. Her shocked exhalation blew warm against his cheek, but he didn't hang around enjoying the sensation. He strode back the way he'd come, and the arms wrapped around his neck tightened their purchase.

It was enough, that one gesture of trust, to ease the chokehold of fear. Enough that he could notice how she wore his shirt and snug white boxers. Enough to register the tickle of a stray curl against his throat, the silken texture of her bare legs against his arm, the soft press of her breasts against his chest.

"I can walk," she said huskily, when he reached the bottom of the stairs. "You don't have to carry me."

"There was glass everywhere."

"Not down here," she pointed out, but her voice shook enough that he held her more tightly to his chest as he made a beeline for his bedroom.

"I'm all right," she said with more force. Then she sucked in a breath. "Where are you taking me?"

About to shoulder open the door to his bathroom, he paused and looked down into her face. "I need to make sure you're all right."

"I am. Really." Except her face was still too pale, her eyes pools of darkness, her voice tremulous. And a deep shudder rolled through her body when she added, "It's just the shock of…of seeing my bed. And all that glass."

Cursing silently, he carried her through the doorway and slid her onto the marble-topped vanity that spanned the width of the room. Briefly he caught his reflection in the mirror at her back. His face looked gaunt, tight, fearsome in its intensity.

Little wonder she'd wanted to be put down. Or that her pulse beat wildly in that vulnerable spot at the base of her throat. In addition to the shock of the branch falling on the bed she'd been about to get into, he'd managed to scare her half to death with his reaction.

"I'm sorry," he murmured gruffly. "Just let me check your feet for splinters—"

"I was in the bathroom. The whole time."

"Show me," he rasped, unwilling and unable to take her word.

He didn't wait for her permission. Setting her hand on his shoulder for balance, he swivelled her on her backside until her legs and bare feet were illuminated by the bright downlights. He heard the shuddery little breath she drew when he took her foot in his hands. Felt the reflexive clutch of her fingers on his shoulder.

And when he looked down at the slender arch of her foot, the delicate bones of her ankle, the pearly colour painted on her nails, he felt a surge of possessiveness so strong it threatened to bring him to his knees. It was partly aftershock of his fear and the panicked rush upstairs, partly the adrenaline surge of acknowledging that she was unharmed. But the other part was raw, primitive desire.

Finally she was here, her skin silky smooth beneath his hands, her legs bare and warm all the way up to *his* boxers.

Bare and warm and shivering, he realised belatedly, and when he put her foot down and swung her back around, he realised that she wore nothing beneath his shirt. Largely unbuttoned, the garment had rucked up and twisted to reveal the rose pink tip of her breast.

She was either very, very cold or very, very turned on.

Van was struck by a wave of yearning. To rip his shirt from her body, to take that breast into his mouth, to feast eyes and mouth and hands on the body he'd once known and could not remember. He forced his hands to pull the shirt back together and set it right, but beneath his fingers the sweet warmth of her body beckoned. He trembled, she trembled—through the roaring in his blood he could not tell which, and when he drew a breath to centre himself, he looked up and caught her eyes on him, intent, unguarded and lambent with the same desire that swamped his senses.

She was trembling. He could feel the delicate tremor in the fingertips still resting on his shoulder. Shock, he told himself.

He picked her up and carried her through to his bed.

He could hold her, just hold and warm and soothe her until she felt safe again. He figured that wouldn't take long. She would realise that this was his bed, his arms around her, that she was burrowing close against him, her nose pressed into the hollow of his throat, his face buried in the fragrant spread of her hair.

She would soon realise that the tight heat of his body was not all about comfort, that he rode a delicate line between restraint and desire.

Then she would know she wasn't safe at all.

But for now…

He lifted a hand and combed the tangle of hair back from her face and she sighed, a soft relenting sound that soothed the jagged edges of his arousal. He pressed his lips to the crown of her head and stroked her back and crooned the words that she needed to hear and the message that he needed to remember.

"It's okay, Susannah. You're safe now. Go to sleep."

Safe, yes, but she was not okay.

When she closed her eyes, her heartbeat scurried like

a frightened rabbit and her only solace was the strong, sure beat of Donovan's heart. One of her hands still clutched at his shirt and she unfurled her fingers to smooth the fabric aside, so she could rest her palm closer to that reassuring pulse.

For a second or two it worked. The other fear faded under the sweet pressure of his lips against her crown, the heat radiating from his body, the stroke of his hands over her back and the thick heartbeat anchoring her in the moment. Then her fingers shifted infinitesimally and she felt the raised scar tissue and everything went completely still.

Him, her, the moment.

No wonder he'd looked so shell-shocked in the bath-room. No wonder he'd needed reassurance of her safety. It wasn't only because he'd brought her here and felt re-sponsible for her safety.

The big hands at her back had stilled and Susannah eased herself up onto her elbow. Enough light bled through the half-open bathroom door for her to see his profile and guarded expression. "Are *you* okay?" she asked.

His jaw tightened. "You're in my bed. I'm very okay."

"You know why I'm asking."

Yes, he knew. That's why he'd made that incendiary comment—to distract her. To stop her asking about something he would see as a vulnerability.

In the shadowy light she caught the glint of danger-ous purpose in his eyes. Felt the shift of pressure in the hand at the base of her spine, felt it like an electric surge of awareness in every female cell.

"I have scars, Susannah," he said, low and dark. "I

had cuts, stitches, multiple surgeries. We can play show-and-tell, if that's what you want, but if you put your hand on my body—anywhere—I'll take that as a sign of different intent."

Susannah looked into his eyes and became lost in an agony of wanting. She ached for those lost weeks, for thinking the worst of him, for not trusting how her heart had first judged him. She knew it was wrong, she knew she would regret it, but she couldn't turn away. She looked at him lying there—white shirt, dark trousers, quicksilver eyes—and her whole being yearned.

She lifted a hand to touch his face and he intercepted its path, held her fingers tight and trembling in his.

"Be very sure, Susannah."

Throat tight with emotion, she nodded. She wanted to say the words, to let him know she'd made this choice, but the affirmation got lost in the flash of his eyes as he took her hand to his mouth and kissed her palm.

Her eyelids drifted closed for that intensely erotic second and then came open again as his hands shifted to her shoulders and turned her onto her back. As he covered her with his body and his kiss.

The completeness of that contact—eyes, lips, bodies—engulfed her in a sweet gulp of heat. She became acutely aware of everywhere they touched. The slow seeking pressure of his lips, the penetrating heat of his hands through the thin fabric of her shirt, the texture of his trousers against her bare thighs.

The slow sweep of his tongue elicited a shudder of response deep in her flesh and she opened her mouth in silent invitation, welcoming him to fill the hollow of her mouth, to drive the last cold fragments of shock from her heart, to reaffirm that he was here and she was safe, that neither of them lay broken and bleeding amid a mountain of splintered glass.

Oh, yes, he was here.

Trailing his mouth along her jawline, nuzzling her neck, gently nipping her earlobe and sucking the pearl stud between his teeth. Her back arched from the mattress, and he whispered something in her ear, a teasing erotic promise that was lost in the elevated rasp of her breath and the swift race of her pulse.

It didn't matter—the words did not matter. It was enough that this was Donovan. The skim of his breath on her sensitive skin, the rough edge to his whisper, the knowing that he—and only he—could bring her body to life and fill the lonely ache of her heart.

And then he was kissing her again, kissing her and sliding his hands down to her hips, melding their bodies as closely as possible without removing the barrier of clothing. For a long moment, she savoured the sensation. Then, with mouths still fused, he rolled to his back and pulled her on top.

This kiss was new again, a wild explosion that fed their greedy passion. His hands on her thighs, on her buttocks, pushing her hard against him—her hands at his shirt, frantic in their haste to bare his chest to the sweet heat of her touch. He relinquished her mouth to nuzzle the fragrant warmth of her throat, to bite the tender skin at the juncture between shoulder and neck.

To absorb the deep-seated quiver of response that wracked her body from fingertips to toes.

"My special spot," she whispered, palming his face. "How did you know? Did you remember?"

Van had acted on raw instinct. He couldn't have known this intensity, this driving need to please her, to spend the rest of his life inside her.

It was completely, terrifyingly new.

To rescue himself from the unknown, he applied himself to what he recognised. Hot swamping desire. He undid the one remaining button on her shirt, exposing her breasts to his eyes. With a long, slow sweep of his tongue he lathed each nipple and then tugged with gentle teeth until she cried out his name.

"Donovan."

He loved his name on her lips, and when she repeated it, her down-under accent penetrated the wall in his mind and echoed through his memory, again and again and again, the breathless cry of a woman's climax.

Driven by a desperate need to hear that same sound now, he flipped her to her back and slid down to stroke the silken skin of her inner thigh. His fingers slipped inside her pants and found her wet and indescribably hot. Beside her hips her fingers clutched at the sheet as if she needed to anchor herself and that sight was powerfully erotic.

Beneath his fingers her body vibrated with the same need that smouldered in her eyes. He didn't need any further explanation or invitation. With quick efficiency he stripped the underwear from her body and then he sat back on his heels to drink in the sight.

Everything from the curve of her elbow to the dip of her waist was a picture of feminine beauty.

His earlier frustration returned with a vicious streak that made him want to howl at the moon. Because for all the glimpses, the flashes, the snaps of sound and image and scent, he couldn't remember this most alluring, transfixing, knock-back-on-his-heels sight.

How could he not remember?

One last time his eyes moved over her, learning that sight, committing every detail to memory, before he rose to his feet and strode to the bathroom to turn out the light.

Susannah had forgotten just how dark it could be in this isolated part of the world, without the constant illumination of a million city lights, without the digital radiance from a score of household electronics.

It was very, very dark.

Last July, they had made love in the dark and in the full light of day. There'd been no cause for modesty at Stranger's Bay and there was definitely no cause here on Charlotte Island. Lying in bed, listening to the sounds of him undressing, Susannah's heart constricted.

Did he really think she would be turned off by his scars?

Did he think her that shallow?

Then she realised that the scars themselves were not the problem, but her reaction to them. With her emotions teetering grimly on the edge of this day's overload, she couldn't guarantee her response. She might go over the top imagining the initial injuries, his pain, his mortality.

She shivered slightly and perhaps she inhaled a gust of air because she sensed his sudden stillness beside the bed. "Does the dark bother you?"

"Only if you can't find me," she said softly.

The mattress dipped under his weight and he was there, causing her heart to skip and her temperature to spike. With one hot hand on her hip, he turned her onto her side, facing him on the big bed.

"I found you."

The simple statement deserved a teasing answer, but Susannah had nothing to offer. He was here, naked, *hers,* and the enormity of that knowledge seeped into every part of her body until she quavered with the intensity of wanting. All she could do was show him, touch him. She skimmed her hands slowly up his arms, over his shoulders, down the long contours of his back.

When she slipped lower, he trapped one of her legs between his and held her firmly in place. Their eyes sought and held despite the darkness, their bodies so close she felt the surge of his response against her belly. Their thighs slid together in a restless dance, and in the beat of a second, the mood had changed, sliced by the edgy hunger in his eyes, in her body, by the growl of his voice.

"I need to be inside you."

Darkness and desire had robbed Susannah of any shyness, and she watched him take care of protection with steady eyes and very unsteady emotions. Then his hand was on her face, touching her lips, asking for her guidance as he settled between her thighs. Their gazes linked as he nudged the entrance to her body, as he started to slide inside, and Susannah forgot everything as longing and loving overlapped in a wave of yearning that claimed her body, mind and her soul.

She welcomed him, hard and strong and vital. There

had only been this man; there could be no other who fit her body, who matched her desire.

His nostrils flared, his gaze gleamed with satisfaction as he filled her to the hilt. He went still and a long, low, pleasured groan escaped his lips and suffused her with the purest bliss. *This is what I lost,* she thought, as they kissed with their eyes open and their bodies joined. They kissed in a rhythm that mimicked the rolling give-and-take of their lower bodies, they kissed until their lungs required sustenance and the sounds of their choppy breathing filled the air.

And just when she thought the exquisite pleasure of his touch could take her no higher, he caught her lower lip between his teeth and stilled. Held rigid over her body, poised on the brink of release, he looked into her eyes and she knew he recognised something in the moment.

She lifted a trembling hand and touched his face, stroked his jaw, and he began to move again, thrusting deep and strong. Susannah hovered, not wanting this over, greedily wanting him there in her body, soaring in this perfect moment forever.

After there would be words, guilt, confessions, and everything would change again.

She wrapped her legs more tightly around him, and that new angle broke both their control. The climax came quickly, catching her in its sweet, savage grip and flinging her high and wild. As she spun out, she chanted his name, a low breathless ache that resounded in her blood and her mind and her heart.

He drove deep one last time and held himself rigid,

straining with the intensity of his own release. With arms and legs and thundering heart, she clung to him, stroking the slick heat of his back and nuzzling her face into his neck, dragging the masculine scent of his body into her lungs and her senses.

Afterward, too, their sated bodies fit together in a perfect melding of hard lines and giving curves. Donovon's arm held her close to his side. His elevated breath on her temple lifted a fine frizz of hair into her vision.

If she had the energy Susannah would have brushed it aside. But she was happily spent, unable to move anything beyond the fingers that traced an indolent pattern across his chest. "Did that trigger your memory?" she asked softly, remembering what she'd seen in his face, what she'd felt in his intensity.

"No."

He sounded relaxed, completely unperturbed, and Susannah's hand stilled. "Doesn't that bug you?"

"Not anymore."

She didn't know what to make of that. Back at Stranger's Bay the frustration of not knowing had reverberated around him like a force field. Beneath her hand she felt the ridged edge of one of the scars that crisscrossed his abdomen. Earlier he'd warned her off asking, but now he was at ease. Now she could ask. "And the attack…does it bother you not remembering how that happened?"

"It bugs me that I was caught out and the bastards got the better of me." The arm at her waist tightened momentarily and Susannah held her breath until he relaxed again. "At least now I see why I might have been distracted."

"By me?"

"By a whole weekend of you. Yeah."

The low rumble of his answer rippled through her, a sweet antithesis to her chilling thoughts about his injuries. "I like the idea that you were thinking of me in your hometown, but I hate what happened because of it."

"The scars?"

"The wounds that caused the scars," she corrected. "What you went through because of them, and everything that happened afterward."

"We can fix that," he said after a moment.

"Can we?"

"Tomorrow."

"And now?"

She felt a change in the mood. The hand at her waist applied a different pressure, a renewed heat, as his fingers splayed wide over her belly. The weight of his legs shifted, pinning her to the bed. "Now—" his voice deepened to a thick growl as he nuzzled her hair from her throat "—I have more memories to replace."

Ten

Van had never been a big sleeper, but for once he welcomed his insomnia. In the pale light of dawn he watched Susannah sleep with a deep-seated satisfaction he'd never felt before...or that he didn't recall feeling before.

And he didn't remember being with her. He hadn't lied about that. All he'd suffered these past days were fleeting impressions, and if anything was capable of blowing those glimpses of the past into fully realised memories then those explosive hours in his bed should have been it.

For once the lack of memory didn't bother him. Now that he'd had her, all he cared about was making sure she stayed. In his bed, in his home, in his life. The permanency of that thought should have scared the hell out of him, but it didn't.

Impatient to move on from the past to a shared future, he left her sleeping and dressed quickly. In the wake of last night's storm, The Palisades' management would send a craft for them. Their seclusion would soon be at an end and he might not get another chance to seek the answers he needed.

He'd walked the island assessing the damage. Seeing the size of the branch that had crashed through the upstairs windows, his gut churned sickly with what might have been. He came in through the back door, and immediately noted the open doors to his bedroom and onto the veranda. She was up. Good.

He crossed the room, finally catching sight of her on the deck. Morning light traced the lines of her body through her shirt and when she lifted a hand to hold her hair back from her face, her striking beauty hit him anew.

His gut tightened with more than morning lust, with more than appreciation of the picture she made. There was something in her body language, in the taut stretch of her neck and the way her hand gripped the balcony rail that spoke of her inner tension and hot-wired straight into his.

In the clear light of morning she wouldn't like what they'd done in the dark of night. He figured she would lay the blame at his feet, but he had no intention of dwelling on culpability. What was done, was done.

He'd brought her here to seduce her, to give her cause to end her marriage plans. That goal had been the farthest thing from his mind last night, but he couldn't pretend to be sorry.

He wondered if Carlisle would be at the resort, awaiting their return. He couldn't believe the man wouldn't be. Or that he wouldn't fight tooth and nail to keep Susannah.

She looked around then, as if the surge of his possessiveness had growled her name. When he approached, she smiled, but the gesture looked as strained and fragile as the shadows of regret in her eyes.

"I saw you out walking," she said, her gaze skating away over the storm-ravaged vista. "There looks to be a lot of trees down. Is there much damage down at the cottage?"

It was a tossup which Van hated more—the recrimination in her eyes, the false cheerfulness in her voice or the fact she'd resorted to small talk. "Are you going to pretend last night didn't happen?" he asked.

She let go of her hair, let the breeze pick it up and screen her face, but that didn't hide the stiffening of her spine. Or the ache of a plea in her response. "For now, yes. I'm not—"

"It has to be now."

She scooped back her hair to reveal wide and wary eyes. "Why?"

"There are boats out on the bay. I imagine one of them is heading our way."

"Oh." Her gaze flickered over him—fully dressed—and then down at her revealing attire. "Then I had better shower and dress."

"After we've talked, Susannah."

He blocked her attempted exit, forced his attention away from the distraction of her nakedness beneath the shirt and waited for her to meet his eyes. The annoyance he saw there was aimed internally, not at him, and the knowledge caused a subtle relenting in his stance.

"Hey," he said softly, "don't beat yourself up." With a gentle hand he threaded her hair behind one ear and held it there, his thumb tracing the tense line of her jaw before touching the pearl in her earlobe. A hot memory of his mouth, right there, rocketed through him and coloured his voice when he added, "It was inevitable."

"No." Shaking her head, she stepped back from his touch and his hand fell away. "You gave me the choice last night. I didn't take it."

"You're here on this island because of me."

"I'm here because I chose to be," she said, her voice choked with the same emotion that darkened her eyes. "I shouldn't have been anywhere near you. I should have stayed in Melbourne. I should have been on my honeymoon."

For several seconds, Van stared at her, unsure if he'd heard correctly. When he realised that the steadily escalating thrum wasn't his heartbeat, he turned and looked out over the bay and saw a helicopter zeroing in on the island. His attention zapped back to Susannah's face. "You're not marrying Carlisle."

"After last night?" Her soft words was barely audible above the *thwap-thwap-thwap* of the helicopter's rotors as it circled overhead, and her eyes swam with the same self-castigation as earlier. "No, I guess I'm probably not."

* * *

Donovan had intimated on the deck at Charlotte Island that they wouldn't be able to talk once the rescue craft arrived. He'd been right. Once back at the resort, solicitous staff hovered over them. A shuttle whisked them to the airport to catch a late-morning flight to Melbourne. It was all so quick and efficient, there'd been little chance for talk until they were seated on the plane. Then his focussed gaze settled on her face and she knew the question of what-now couldn't be avoided any longer.

Tilting her face, she turned to meet his eyes. "What happens when we get back to Melbourne?"

"We sort out the contract on The Palisades. Then we talk—" he leaned closer, tapped the back of her hand with his finger "—about us."

Susannah's heart kicked up a beat and she had to caution herself not to leap into the promise of those words. First she needed to sort out her agreement with Alex. Then there was her business, which could choke and die without an urgent injection of funds.

"I'm meeting with Armitage this afternoon," he said.

Wow. He hadn't wasted any time getting back to business. She didn't even know when he'd found time to make the phone call to Horton's CEO. The pleasurable ripple he'd started in her veins with his talk of *us* braked to a sudden halt. "So soon?" she asked. "Shouldn't you at least wait until I've spoken to Alex?"

"I need to set things in motion before I leave."

She straightened, her gaze springing up to meet his. "You're leaving? *When?*"

"That depends on this meeting, but as soon as possible?"

"Because of Mac?" she guessed.

The attendant interrupted with a polite admonishment, drawing their attention to the pre-flight safety instruction. Staring blindly at the video screen, Susannah digested this news. She hadn't considered that he might be leaving so swiftly. She hadn't allowed herself to think beyond—

"Come with me."

His voice, low and intense, was close to her ear. Had she heard him correctly? Startled, she looked around and found those eyes—silver, sharp, determined—focussed on hers. Her heart gave an excited bump. "I can't. I have to talk to Alex, and there's my business. I can't just drop everything and leave."

"You weren't going to do that for this honeymoon you mentioned?"

"Yes, but…" Her voice trailed off as her gaze slid back to the screen. A honeymoon was two weeks. He was asking her to… She didn't know what *come with me* implied. "Can we talk about this after I've talked to Alex?"

"When?"

"I don't know. As soon as I can."

He fell silent, leaving her to spend the rest of the flight worrying over that upcoming conversation. Donovan had told her not to beat herself up, but how could she not? She'd acted dishonourably, without willpower, and she took ownership of that choice. She refused to blame it on fear or adrenaline or the need to affirm life.

Now she had to tell Alex that the temporary delay on their wedding plans was permanent.

She couldn't marry him, not when another man lay claim to her heart.

Her mother met the flight, her reception for Donovan a chilling contrast to her effusive embrace of Susannah. Out of politeness Miriam offered him a lift to the city, which he declined with a pointed, "I prefer to make my own plans."

"Call me," he told Susannah, and she read the unsaid rest in his eyes. *After you've talked to Carlisle.* Watching him walk away without once looking back, his stride long and purposeful, she felt a panicky sense of loss. That fear—that emotion—must have been written all over her face because her mother tsked her disapproval. "Oh, Susannah, didn't you learn the last time?"

"I don't know what you're talking about."

"You can try to fool me, darling, but please don't fool yourself." Her mother spoke briskly, but the look she turned on Susannah brimmed in castigation. "He used you the first time and he's used you again."

Susannah's stride faltered. "What do you mean by that?" she asked, hurrying to catch up.

"Do you know he's meeting with Horton's this afternoon? He called the minute he got off the island, wanting to talk deals. According to Judd, he's very confident that Carlisles won't go ahead with the purchase of The Palisades. Does that mean you've changed your mind about marrying Alex?"

Susannah nodded and although her mother frowned, she didn't break stride until they reached her Mercedes. "Aren't you going to try and talk me out of this rash and foolish decision?" Susannah asked across the roof of the car.

"Unfortunately I agree with you. You can't marry him."

Susannah blinked in surprise. "I thought you were set on having a Carlisle for a son-in-law."

"I was, but…" She made a dismissive gesture, her expression tight. "Never mind."

But Susannah did mind, and once they were cruising south on the freeway, she turned toward her mother. "What aren't you telling me? What shouldn't I mind?"

"Some things are better left unknown."

"I am twenty-eight years old. Please, don't keep anything from me for my own good."

"Very well," Miriam said stiffly after a moment's consideration. "I wasn't going to tell you, but I suppose it may come out anyway. Lord knows why this hasn't been splashed around the gossip sheets already."

"Do you mean Donovan and me? I don't think—"

"No, not you. Alex Carlisle. He spent the weekend with another woman."

Susannah's mouth opened but no sound came out. She shut it. Shook her head. Tried again. "No. Not Alex. He wouldn't."

"I saw them, outside the Carlisle Grande on Sunday afternoon. The woman was blond, tall, very distinctive in a common sort of way. She was riding a motorcycle." Miriam all but sniffed with disdain. "He kissed her, right there under the hotel *porte cochere*. In broad daylight, for anyone to see, and I am not talking a sisterly peck. This was a long and indiscreet embrace. I'm sorry, darling, but can you see why I wasn't going to tell you?"

Struggling to digest the information, Susannah didn't answer. Alex and Zara? No, not possible. Although she had sent her sister to deliver her message to the hotel. And it would explain why Alex hadn't called or tried to track her down. If this were true, then backing out of her marriage agreement might not be as difficult as she'd imagined.

"Are you sure it was Alex?" she asked slowly.

"It was Alex. Now," Miriam continued briskly, "about this Donovan Keane. Do you love him?"

What was the point in prevaricating? Her mother had read the truth in her face at the airport, when she'd watched him walk away. "I wouldn't have gone to Tasmania if I didn't."

"That's what I feared."

Susannah sat up straight. "Don't pass judgment, Mother. You don't know him. You don't know what he's been through or how badly he wants The Palisades."

"Oh, I think I do." There was something in her mother's frown, in the dark look she slid Susannah's way, that stopped Susannah's heart for a second. "The question is, how badly do *you* want him?"

Coming to Donovan's hotel was not the smartest thing Susannah had ever done. She should have taken time to think, to let the dust settle, to gain a better perspective than her gut reaction to what her mother had revealed.

So here she was, sitting in the foyer of the Lindrum, waiting for Donovan to pick up his room phone. When it switched to voice mail, she closed her eyes in dismay. Was this to be the story of her life?

Susannah Horton lived to a grand old age of ninety-eight. Lamentably, half those years were spent narrating messages and waiting for the calls to be returned.

Where was he? During the taxi ride from her South Yarra duplex, she'd calmed her nerves by setting the scene in her imagination.

She would call his room, he would answer, she would say, "I need to see you," he would say, "Come on up," and—

"Susannah?"

She came to her feet in a rush, her heart doing a joyous dance of welcome even though she cautioned it to behave. "I was just calling your room."

"I'm not there."

No, he was here.

Looking altogether too gorgeous, damn him, in a dark suit and tie. His gaze drifted over her, taking in the shoes, the stockings, the dress. The hair she'd groomed to within an inch of its natural life.

Nerves fluttered in her belly, but she felt immensely pleased that he was noticing. She might have been miffed with him, but that hadn't prevented her spending significant time deciding on the little black dress and even longer primping.

"When I saw you sitting here, I hoped to see luggage at your side. This—" his gaze skimmed the dress before returning to her face "—looks more like a dinner date than travelling."

"Sorry to disappoint."

"I'm not too disappointed, except if I'd known you were here waiting, I wouldn't have let the meeting drag so long."

Exactly the reminder she'd needed of why she was here. She drew a quick breath and fixed him a cool glare. "I'm surprised the meeting dragged, given how you went in there with such a set idea of what you wanted."

The lazy drift of his eyes steadied on hers. "News travels fast at Horton's."

"When you talk to Judd Armitage about anything that concerns a Horton, my mother will hear."

"Do I take it you have a problem with the deal I'm brokering?"

"You don't think you should have run your *deal* by me first?" she asked, unable to keep the indignation from her voice. "Perhaps you might even have waited until I was un-engaged."

"I don't have time to sit around cooling my heels. I needed to get started," he said evenly. "Today was to open negotiations."

"By requesting the same deal, the same terms, as Alex?"

He regarded her narrowly for a moment. "As I said, a starting point."

Susannah choked out a laugh and shook her head. "Why would I agree to another contract marriage?" she asked, holding out her hands in mock appeal. "Why would you even contemplate something like that?"

"Why," he countered after a heartbeat of silence, "are you so opposed to the concept?"

Although his expression was fixed, his voice even, there was something in his stillness that caused her heart to kick in, hard.

"You intended marrying Carlisle," he continued. "If I hadn't reappeared, you would have married him last Saturday. I can only surmise that your objection is to marrying me."

Marry Donovan? Her heart beat hard and fast with the possibility, until she needed to draw a deep breath to settle the giddiness. "With Alex, I knew exactly what was going on."

"And you wanted to marry him."

"Yes, I did. I wanted everything the marriage offered."

"Which begs the question, what part of *everything* can't I offer? It's not the money or the business rescue package. I know it's not the sex." He paused long enough for their gazes to catch and cling in a shimmer of remembered heat, before continuing in the same deceptively level tone. "Is it the Carlisle name? Or the big, happy family?" When she didn't answer right away, he leaned closer, and anger flashed brief and hot in his eyes. "Why him, Susannah, and not me?"

"Because he asked," she replied, her voice thick with the same heat. "It was that easy, Donovan. He didn't take a deal to Horton's because he was impatient. Yes, he was in a hurry, too, but he didn't pick the easiest course to expedite matters. He asked me and he gave me time to consider the offer."

"And yet you didn't go ahead with it...."

"Right now," she fired back, "I'm wondering why I didn't!"

For a long moment, they faced off. The intensity of her angry words still buzzed through Susannah's veins and clouded her vision. So much so that she didn't notice the approach of the front-desk manager until he cleared his throat.

"Excuse me, Mr. Keane."

Intent on their exchange, she'd forgotten all about their surroundings, but now she glanced around. Thankfully the public lobby was deserted apart from the manager, now engaged in conversation with Donovan.

"A phone call," he was saying, sotto voce. "A Ms. O'Hara. She said to find you if at all possible. An emergency. You can use my office—it's over here."

Donovan turned back to Susannah. A distracted frown drew his brows together as he checked his watch. "I need to take this."

"I'll wait."

She sensed he might suggest otherwise, but then he simply nodded. As she watched him stride away, Susannah did the time translation. It was very early in the morning in California, surely too early for his assistant—she recognized the name, after all those stonewalled calls she'd made back in July—to be calling on business.

By the time Donovan came out of the manager's office, she'd circled the foyer on anxious feet a dozen times. One look at his tightly drawn features confirmed her worse fears. "Is it Mac?" she asked, intercepting his long-striding path.

"She's been taken to hospital," he told her, not easing

his pace until he reached the lifts. He punched the up button with controlled aggression. "I'm leaving as soon as possible."

Susannah didn't need to ask for details. The answer hummed in the tightly leashed tendons of his neck, in the jump of a muscle in his jaw. "What can I do to help?" she asked. "I can call the airlines, book you flights."

"That isn't necessary."

"It's what I do," she pointed out. "I can ensure you're on the earliest flight to San Francisco, whether that's from Melbourne or Sydney or Auckland or—"

"Thank you, but Erin is on that." His tone clipped and final, was punctuated by the electronic ping that signaled the lift's arrival. The doors slid open. "This is why I needed to get things moving," he said tightly. "Before it's too late."

"I'll talk to Alex and to Judd. I'll make sure you get the same deal as your initial bid."

Inside the car, he turned and their eyes met—one second where the shutters slid aside to reveal a storm of emotion. One second for Susannah to realise, with a blinding flash of belated clarity, that she'd said the worst possible thing. She'd confirmed his belief that she didn't want to marry him.

Eleven

The rain came with the night, a downpour that blocked Van's view of the bay and trapped him inside with only the bleakness of his thoughts for company.

This afternoon he'd said his last goodbye to Mac in a short, private funeral service. Afterward he'd returned to the Sausalito apartment he'd rented after his hospital stay.

He would have been happy with a hotel suite close to to Keane MacCreadie's offices, but Mac had found and organised the rental. She'd spouted the benefits of relaxing water views, the bayside walks and a nearby health club. Van relented because Mac lived close by and those visits made the inconvenience worthwhile.

Except there'd not been nearly enough visits. A handful of weeks where he'd pushed himself harder than his physio advised in order to recover his physical strength. The rest researching the deal gone wrong in preparation for his second trip down under.

A trip rendered meaningless by Mac's death. She'd passed peacefully—for that, he thanked God—and without regaining consciousness. Van had been too late to say goodbye, his grief at the loss weighed down with the knowledge that he'd failed her.

He'd spent too many precious days in Australia. Day one he could have tied up the deal if he'd not bent his initial plan of swift vengeance. All because he'd wanted Susannah Horton warm and willing in his bed.

He should have been home; he should have been here for Mac; he was the only family she'd had.

The opera playing while he cooked ended in a blistering crescendo of angst, the perfect accompaniment to an untouched dinner and his dark mood. As he crossed to select a more soothing sound track the doorbell rang. He stopped, frowning at the prolonged strident sound. It crossed his mind that someone was leaning on the thing, and could have been doing so for some time. Lord knows, he wouldn't have heard.

It also crossed his mind to ignore it. He wasn't expecting visitors—since he didn't share this address, he never did. But curiosity got the better of him, and he started for the door.

At first he thought there was no one there. Kids pranking, although it was a helluva night for it. Searching for any sign of mischief he glared out through the rain, and on the very edge of the glow cast by his porch light he caught a sign of movement.

The sheen of an ivory raincoat, a yellow umbrella halted and then spun in the light.

Van's heart jerked, his pulse rate rocketing even while his brain rejected the notion. She couldn't be here. Not after their acrimonious parting in Melbourne a week ago.

But she was very much here, scurrying down his path in those familiar skinny-heeled boots.

The bottom of the coat blew open, flashing stockinged knee and thigh and the heat of memory raced through Van's blood. Unwanted but not unwelcome. Suddenly the prospect of her company wasn't so bad. He was in the perfect mood for a confrontation.

She came to a stop under the shelter of the porch, and when she lowered the umbrella the light turned her hair into a fiery nimbus. A tentative smile curved her lips and Van's need of that warmth, that quiet fire, slammed into him like a freight train.

"We seem to have some sort of cosmic connection with the rain," she said, shaking a spray of raindrops from her sleeve. Then she saw his face and the smile in her eyes clouded over. "I'm sorry. I didn't mean to sound so…blithe."

She huffed out a breath and shook her head, and Van let the uncomfortable moment stretch. He hated that a part of him yearned to ease the moment, to bring the smile back to her face. Another part of him wanted to walk back inside, to slam the door in her face, to shut out this fierce raft of emotions she elicited simply by being here. Simply by being *her*.

A larger part ached to pull her inside with him, to turn

her against the door, to unbutton her coat and appease the cold torment of this day in the heat of her body.

"I knew this would be awkward, just arriving on your doorstep—"

"Then why didn't you call?" he asked.

"I tried, several times. You're either not answering your private phone or screening my calls. Erin was kind enough to give me your address."

Erin, kind? Van's brows rose at that oxymoron. "Are you sure you had the right Erin?"

Their eyes met for a second, hers ridiculously pleased by this small sign of relenting. "Yay tall—" she demonstrated with her free hand "—dark hair, pretty eyes. Unfriendly, until I let her know why I wanted your address."

"Did it cross your mind that I might not be home?"

"I saw your lights and heard the music before I let the cab leave."

"And if I hadn't opened the door?"

"That did cross my mind," she admitted. "I went out to see if the cab was still lurking and then your outside light came on." And despite his unwelcoming stance— or perhaps because of it—she drew herself up tall and added, "But I would have called back tomorrow."

"Why would you do that?"

She looked away, her lips pressed together as if she was gathering her composure. And, damn, when she looked back up the green gleam of moisture turned her eyes luminous in the porch light. "You know why."

Yeah, he knew why, but the pull of those tears and the husky edge to her voice twisted him inside out.

"I'm so sorry to hear about Mac."

She took a step toward him, but Van kept her at bay with the cool bite of his words. "I gathered you heard. Unfortunate timing, wasn't it?"

Her head came up, her eyes widening with a combination of hurt and confusion. "I came as soon as I could."

"Really?" The raw remains of the past five days, the guilt, the recrimination, the futility—the wanting her quiet strength beside him—burned like acid. "You've wasted your time. Now Mac's gone, I have no reason to go ahead with the purchase of The Palisades. I don't need anything from you."

Susannah knew she'd taken a big risk. She'd made another of those snap decisions that had gotten her into trouble before, another decision driven by her heart. Despite the coldness of his greeting, she still believed it was the right choice.

Today he'd buried his mentor, business partner, grandmother—the one person he would do anything for—and that grief was etched in every harsh line of his face. If he was trying to shut everyone out as Erin had intimated, if that was his way of dealing with the wretchedness of his loss, then he would have to work a darn sight harder.

Chin high and eyes steady on his, she stood her ground. "I'm not leaving, Donovan. I'm not here about the contract; I'm here for you. Tonight I thought you could use a friend."

"Friends?" He exhaled on a humourless laugh. "Is that how you see us?"

"I thought we were more." Outside in the street a car

horn blared, a distraction that lifted his narrow-eyed gaze from her face and a reminder that they hadn't progressed past his doorstep. "I thought we'd passed the stage of conversing on the porch, at any rate. Aren't you going to invite me inside?"

For a moment she thought he might deny her even that, but then he opened the door and held out his arm in a go-right-ahead gesture. The steely glint in his eyes was not so welcoming. A chill that had nothing to do with the rainy night shivered up Susannah's spine as she took her first tentative steps across the threshold and into his home.

"Can I take your coat?"

The door closed with a thud and Susannah's nerves jumped. Her fingers stuttered over the belt and buttons. Then she felt him close behind her, hands at her shoulders, helping off her coat.

"Thank you," she murmured, looking around.

This was his home—temporary home, she reminded herself, but still she wanted to see. Outside she'd been consumed by nerves and by the angst of the music that soared from inside. Her only impression was of stucco and terra cotta and now she noticed that the Mediterranean theme continued inside. White textured walls, arched openings between the rooms, woven mats and potted palms and bold splashes of red, gold and black in the furnishings.

She was drawn irresistibly toward the kitchen and the redolent scent of cooking. Nerves stirred to life by the dangerous look in his eyes when she came through the door calmed under the memory of their last night at

Charlotte Island, the camaraderie they'd shared working shoulder to shoulder.

"Whatever you are cooking smells delicious."

Hoping to identify the dish, she inhaled deeply and realised that the meaty richness was underlaid with sweetness. Then she caught sight of a sheath of flowers on the low table. White lilies. All the calm and comfort punched from her body.

She turned on her heel, found Donovan still by the door, watching her with a darkly hooded gaze. "I'm so sorry," she said quickly. "I didn't realise when you left Melbourne that she had so little time left."

"No one did."

"Not even you?"

"Do you think I'd have taken the trip to Australia and wasted days at the island if I'd known."

The low, harsh pronouncement echoed in Susannah's heart. On top of everything else, he was lamenting those days they'd spent together. "Those days weren't wasted," she said.

"Days spent chasing a meaningless deal?"

"No, not meaningless. How can you think that? You took the trip because of Mac, to return the place she held so dearly to her ownership. Do you think she would have wanted you to abandon that? Wouldn't she have wanted to see Charlotte Island back in MacCreadie hands?"

"I'm not a MacCreadie," he said harshly.

"Is that what Mac thought? You told me the lengths she went to in finding you. She admitted the truth after years of maintaining her silence about your blood relationship. Of course she saw you as family. Tell me, if the acquisition had gone through after July, if you'd been successful in your bid that time, what would have happened now? Who would she have left the place to?"

"I'm her sole heir." Said as though that was unwanted, unwarranted, unwelcome.

Susannah understood. She ached with his hurt and his anger at being robbed all over again. He didn't want Mac's estate, he wanted time to give back something of what she'd given him. "I understand how much Mac meant to you and how you must be feeling—"

"Do you, do you have any notion what it's like to have no one who believes in you but this one woman who was prepared to back me with everything she owned? Do you know what it's like to spend thirty years not knowing where you came from, to find the answers and the family and then to lose it all weeks later?

"Hell, Susannah, I wasn't even here for her. The one time she needed me, I wasn't here."

The low fervour of his words resonated between them in the quiet. Susannah had no words, no response. His wretchedness pierced her. She wanted nothing more than to cross the space that separated them, to wrap her arms around him, to comfort him with the knowledge that he wasn't alone. That he hadn't lost the only person who loved him. But he kept her at bay with the barrier of his stance and the hostility in his eyes.

"Have you looked at this from Mac's perspective?" she asked, "Or only from your own?"

His features tightened. "Mac died alone," he said bluntly. "That's the perspective I'm seeing."

Oh, Donovan. She hadn't realised. When he didn't answer his phone, she'd imagined him at Mac's bedside. She'd hoped he'd had some time, that he'd at least arrived in time to say goodbye. "I didn't know. I'm so sorry."

He didn't respond, but she could see the muscle working in his jaw. He abandoned the position he'd maintained just inside the room—close to the door, as if he'd not yet decided whether to let her stay or to open that door and order her out—and stalked across to arched windows overlooking the bay.

"From another perspective," she continued carefully, "I imagine Mac was inordinately proud of your success. She wouldn't have invested everything in you, back in those early years, if she hadn't believed in you. And she wouldn't have trusted you with her secrets or with her inheritance if she hadn't trusted and loved you."

"She still died alone."

"No, Donovan. She was alone before she found you. She died knowing she had a grandson who loved her, who I imagine was here for her in all manner of ways these past years."

For a long moment, he stared blindly out into the darkness before he could answer. "Never enough," he said gruffly. "Business, travel, I was never here enough."

In the glass Van saw her approach, the reflected movement of her hair and the blue-green dress that skimmed the lines of her body. He wanted to focus on those curves, the legs, the physical memory of her skin bare and sleek and giving beneath his. But that gave way to a hammering need for her arms, her comfort, the steady strength of her gaze on his as she told him she was here for him.

It was too much, too intense, and Van took a mental step back. Again he'd revealed too much, exposed himself too readily. With this woman it was too easy, and she'd done nothing to earn such trust.

She paused at his side. He could sense her composing herself, preparing her next pretty—and futile—attempt to console him. When she placed her hand on his shoulder, he felt the hot jolt of response and the more powerful underlying need for more.

"If you really want to make me feel better," he said, "the bedroom's right through that archway over there."

"Will that make you feel better?"

"I sure as hell won't feel any worse."

"Okay," she said after a beat of pause, surprising the hell out of him. "If that's what it takes."

Van turned his narrowed gaze on her. "Takes to what?"

"To accept that I'm here for you."

He knew what he should have done. He should have stopped this conversation with his mouth on hers. He should have taken the soft hand that dropped away and put it back on his body. Somewhere infinitely more volatile than his shoulder.

He should have been unzipping the prim and proper dress and pulling aside her lacy underthings to get to the improper. Right here, against that glass.

But, damn her, with that one simple statement, she'd refired his earlier distrust about her reason for coming here and he couldn't let that go. "You say you're here for me—" he turned to meet her eyes more fully "—but what about your own interests?"

Confusion clouded her expression and the tone of her reply. "My…interests?"

"You and your mother and the Horton company stand to lose significantly if you can't talk me into reevaluating The Palisades deal. You've lost Alex Carlisle as a buyer and as a husband. It can't be easy to find buyers who are willing to be screwed around over contract clauses."

"That isn't fair," she countered, eyes sparking green in the low light. "You asked for the extra clauses. That wasn't our doing."

"I only asked for the same as Carlisle. Nothing more, nothing less."

"You didn't ask *me*."

When she started to turn away, he stopped her. With a hand on each arm, he swung her back to the window and blocked her exit path with his body. There were too many questions still unanswered to let her escape. "Why Carlisle? What was the real attraction, Susannah?" When she didn't answer right away, he leaned in closer, his gaze on the curve of her lips. "You hadn't even kissed him, and you were going to—"

"I told you last week. He offered everything I wanted. Everything *and* a baby."

Even as the words left her tongue, Susannah wished them back. She saw their impact, felt the tensing of his hands on her shoulders for a half second before he asked, "You were marrying him to have a baby?"

"He was marrying *me* to have a baby," she corrected. Then, when he continued to study her in unnerving silence, she added, "That may sound like semantics, but it's a significant difference. Alex needed a baby for his family to inherit from his father's will."

"A fine reason to plan a baby."

"He was motivated as you were—by a person he would do anything for. In Alex's case, his mother."

"I was pursuing a piece of land," he said tightly, "not a child."

How could she have not realised what a hot-button issue this would be?

She had to explain, to make him understand…. "This baby was not just a pawn, Donovan. We both wanted a family—not just one child but siblings who would grow up together and fight and love and be there for each other. A family like the Carlisles, who would do anything for each other. It wasn't about the money or the name. It was about family and me turning twenty-nine and the assumption I made when you didn't return my calls."

His gaze narrowed sharply. "What does this have to do with me?"

Susannah's heart thudded hard and high in her throat. She could see no other option but to tell him everything. Including the most wrenching regret of all.

Twelve

"Have you ever wondered why I was calling you? Why I kept calling? Why I was so desperate to reach you even though I thought you were skiving me off?"

Donovan went still. Very still. "You were pregnant?"

She nodded, then had to swallow a choking knot of emotion before she could speak. "For a very short time. Yes."

"I didn't use protection?"

"We used condoms, but the last time…there was a possibility."

He studied her for a long second before swinging away. In stunned silence he stared out into the darkness, his profile harsh and forbidding. Susannah could only imagine what he must be feeling. Shock, disbelief, the impotence of realising what might have been.

"Did I know? Did I promise to call you?"

"Yes."

"Except I didn't and I couldn't take your calls." Finally he turned, and the impact of his next words struck as cold and hard as hailstones. "And Carlisle arrived at the perfect time with the perfect arrangement, for you and my baby."

"No!" Susannah shook her head vehemently. "I'd been trying to contact you, trying to work out what to do if you didn't want to know, and then I miscarried and I realised just how much I'd wanted that baby. That's when Alex asked. That's why I was so open to his suggestion."

"To his suggestion that you conceive another baby? Tell me, is that like hopping back on a bike after you've fallen off? Better done straight away before you forget how?"

"No," she choked out, appalled by that callous analogy. "I wouldn't marry him straight away. I asked for more time. I didn't sleep with him."

"You wanted a wedding ring on your finger this time?"

"I wanted time to reconsider, to think everything through when I wasn't feeling so hollow and hopeless. I wanted to be sure my reasoning was valid and not just an emotional backlash to my loss. I needed to be sure."

"Sure of what?" For the first time his icy control cracked, revealing the fierce churn of anger in his eyes. "That you wanted a baby? It didn't matter if it was his or mine, if your relationship was based on love or greed or a wad of contract pages. You wanted for *you*. You didn't give a flying thought about the baby or how he'd come to view his parents' relationship."

"That's not true. We had solid reasons—"

"So solid you ran away from your wedding day. So solid you spent your honeymoon in my bed."

Reeling from the sustained force of his words, Susannah struggled to hold her head high. To keep the gathering tears at bay. "You know why I came to Tasmania."

"Because I threatened your sham of a wedding…or because you wanted a ready excuse not to see it through?"

"Because you called, because I heard your voice on the phone, because I couldn't help myself," she countered, her voice resonant with the force of her denial. "Damn you, Donovan, I didn't just fall into your bed. You were there. You know that."

"Why did you sleep with me?"

"For the same reason I came here today, the same reason I didn't take the hint on the porch when you tried to freeze me out. The same reason I'm standing here arguing the point about something you're not willing to hear. Because I love you."

"You love me?" He expelled a gust of pure cynicism. "Yet you won't have a bar of a contract that ties you to me?"

"I don't want to be tied to you by business," she stormed back. "With Alex it didn't matter, with you everything has mattered. Everything is amplified. The brief elation when I thought I was having your baby. Not being able to contact you and realising you'd used me that weekend, that you weren't going to be quite so overjoyed by my news. I had the perfect marriage—the perfect future—planned until you came back."

Resistance screamed from every taut line of his body,

and she wondered if anything she'd said had infiltrated that shuttered barrier. Anything that had, he didn't believe…or he didn't want to believe. To Susannah, suddenly it didn't matter which.

She'd tried to explain why she'd found Alex's offer of marriage so hard to refuse. If he didn't accept any of that, how could she convince him of something as inexplicable as her love?

"I know this wasn't the best time to bare my soul," she told him. "That's not why I came here. This wasn't supposed to be about me or my feelings, but now you know everything and I'm not sorry it's been said."

"Why didn't you tell me before?"

"Maybe I knew it would lead to this."

For a moment the antagonism of *this* arced between them, and it was too much. Before he could say any more, she shook her head in warning. "I think we've both said enough for now. I'll call a cab."

"You drop that series of bombshells and that's it?"

"Until we've both cooled down and reflected, yes."

"You need to think some more? To change your mind again? To decide whether this really is true love?"

Susannah had no answer to the cruel slice of those questions. She'd had enough. She couldn't stand here while he ripped apart her avowal of love, while he mocked the heartfelt decisions she'd made these past months. She was walking away while she still had some dignity. Before the tears commenced.

With trembling fingers she pulled her phone from her bag. She'd saved the number, if only she could stop her hands shaking enough to punch the right keys…

"There's no need to call a cab. Where are you staying?"

"The Carlisle."

His mouth tightened into a grim line. "I'll drive you."

She wanted to tell him where to put that offer—but she refused to gift him the pleasure of another argument. Ever since she arrived, he'd been pushing for a confrontation. Perhaps, like a wounded animal, he'd needed to latch out at the pain caused by Mac's loss. Naively, she'd obliged, thinking she could absorb some of that hurt with her love. Now she'd had enough.

In the car, she closed her eyes and shut him out—gathering the silence around her like a cloak as his powerful car sliced through the wet night. At the hotel, he came around to open her door, and she was forced to meet his eyes for the first time since he'd ushered her from his home...and to face the fact that this might be goodbye.

In that moment all her bravado turned to water. She couldn't look him in the eye and brazen it out. Nor could she turn and walk away with nothing.

It was easier—so much easier—to lean into his body and kiss his cheek. She felt his stillness, the tension in his jaw and the whisker-rough texture of his skin beneath her lips. Her fingers curled briefly around his lapel, a last touch, a last deep breath of his scent. "Take care," she said quickly. There was no point in saying keep in touch or call me. She'd done that twice, to no avail. "I'm sorry for your loss."

And as she went to pull away, his hand came up and grabbed her arm. Their eyes met for a quicksilver moment. "I'm sorry for yours, Susannah. I wish you hadn't had to go through that on your own."

The rush of tears at the back of her eyes was instant, overwhelming, but if she let one free she feared they would never stop. With a brief nod of acknowledgment, she pulled free and somehow managed to walk away with her head held high.

"Will you just take the damn call?" Erin's voice came through the speakerphone in measured bites of aggravation. "This is your business, your deal, she can't put you in any worse a mood then we've suffered these past weeks!"

Van figured the call had to be from Horton's about The Palisades. *She* had to be Miriam Horton. And his assistant made a valid point—he was in the perfect mood for this call. "Put it through," he said shortly, his gaze still fixed on the opening charts for today's trading.

"Hello, Donovan? It's Susannah."

Van jerked upright in his chair, his jaw flexed and tight at the unexpected greeting. All the air left his lungs as if he'd been punched. He'd not expected to hear from her, not after the finality of their parting. So many times he'd thought about calling, but what the hell would he say? He didn't know how to make things right. If he couldn't give her *everything* she wanted, what could he offer?

"Donovan? Are you there?"

With a rough note of disgust, he picked up the receiver. Since the memory of her voice was constantly in his head, he might as well enjoy the real thing in his ear. "Susannah, yeah, I'm here." He checked his watch and felt a jab of alarm. "It's the middle of the night in Melbourne. Is everything all right?"

"I'm…not home."

Van sat up straighter. It had been almost two weeks but… "Are you still here, in San Francisco?"

"No," she said quickly. Too quickly. "I'm in the mountains. Since I'd arranged time away from the office, I thought I might as well take a holiday."

What the hell was he supposed to say to that? *Hope you're having a nice time on what was supposed to be your honeymoon. Wish I was there.* "To do some thinking?" he bit out.

There was a beat of silence, long enough for him to call himself an ass for pressing that hot button. "Yes, as a matter of fact. Walking up here is very good for clearing the mind and thinking."

"On the island you told me you weren't a fan of exercise."

"I'm not but I do need to work on my core strength," she said with an irony that suggested she was talking about more than physical strength. "But I didn't call to talk about me."

"No?"

"I spoke to my mother about the contract for The Palisades. I wanted you to know that Judd will be calling about new terms, in line with your original bid."

"Can't find another buyer?" he asked.

"I don't believe that will be a problem, but you deserve first offer."

"I told you I was no longer interested."

"And I hope you've reconsidered." She drew an audible breath, the gesture so familiar he could picture the exact look on her face. The way her chin came up a fraction. The cool green flash of her eyes. "I don't think you're foolish enough to allow your opinion of me to influence your decision, but be assured I have no personal agenda."

"You just wanted to be sure I didn't sign the old version?"

"Exactly."

"What about your business?" he found himself asking. "Do you still need equity capital?"

"I've just come to terms with my mother. She now owns a managing share in At Your Service."

"I'm sorry to hear that."

"Why should you be?" she replied tersely. "She has some excellent ideas for diversifying and making the business more profitable."

Van wanted to ask about *her* vision, about the pride she'd taken in her own direction without her parents' controlling hand, but he bit down on the urge. Satisfied another urge by asking, "And what about the other clause in the old contract?"

"I'm sorry?"

"What if I want you as my wife?"

One swift inhalation in his ear. One second of pure what-the-hell-are-you-asking fear, before his heartbeat settled into a slow and certain rhythm.

"You don't," she rasped out.

"I asked for the same terms as Carlisle."

"Because you wanted to expedite matters. You never wanted anything but that contract."

"No, Susannah, I wanted you." With the phone clutched to his ear, he shoved to his feet and paced to the window. A magnificent view of city and bay stretched before him, unseen, unacknowledged. All he could see was her face, her smile, her wild hair and sea-green eyes. "You said you love me."

"I do," she said sadly, "but that's not enough."

"Because I can't give you that perfect future you had all mapped out?"

"I thought you could, but maybe I was wrong. Maybe I deserve better." Her voice lifted on that last statement and he pictured her chin rising with it. "Goodbye, Donovan, and good luck with Judd. I hope that works out for you. Charlotte Island was meant to be yours."

There was nothing he could do to stop her disconnecting, but the conversation played through his mind, the words exactly as they'd sounded in his ear. The honey-dipped tone of her voice. The distinctive down-under accent. The snotty edge when she told him that maybe she deserved better.

For several seconds, he entertained the notion that she did deserve better. She'd walked away from a marriage she believed could give her everything. She'd flown halfway around the world to offer her support. She'd told him she loved him and he'd fobbed that off, too intent on licking his wounds and protecting himself from another round of love and loss to accept the honesty of that gift.

He couldn't blame her for thinking she deserved better. He wouldn't blame her if she refused to listen to what he had to say. But he would say it—everything that needed to be said, everything that he'd gotten so wrong the first time.

Then she could decide what *he* deserved.

* * *

Damn weather. Susannah swung at the moving target and missed. *Damn punching bag.* She hit out again, this time connecting with an audible thud that jarred through her gloved fist all the way to her shoulder. *Damn man.*

She unleashed a wild series of punches. Some of them actually found purchase on the hunk of leather. More didn't. But there was enough satisfaction in the occasional thud to keep her swinging for several more minutes, until her breath grew short and ragged and her muscles ached from exertion.

Dodging the wildly undulating bag, she pulled off her gloves and reached for her towel and water. A quick cooldown on the treadmill and then she would treat her well-used muscles to a long, soothing bath. The prospect almost brought a smile to her mouth as she turned toward the door.

And then she saw him. Leaning against the wall just inside the door of the Tahoe resort's fitness center. Dark suit, white shirt, silver-grey eyes riveting her to the spot as he straightened.

Everything inside her went still as he closed the space between them with slow, sure footsteps. As he approached, she could feel him taking in the yoga pants and crop top, which made her look the part, and the new haircut. The shortened curls were still unruly, despite the sweatband that was supposed to keep them secured.

"Hello, Susannah." He stopped in front of her, close enough that she could see the softening mix of amusement and appreciation in his eyes. "I like the new look. It suits you."

"I think so." Their gazes met and held in a moment's assessment, but that was all Susannah allowed herself. He'd tracked her down less than a day after that phone conversation, but she hardened her heart against its foolish leap of hope. "You're a long way from home," she said coolly.

"I have unfinished business."

"How did you know where to find me?" A frown creased her brow as she considered the possibilities. "My mother is the only person—" Seeing the answer in his eyes, she stopped. "*Miriam* told you where I was staying?"

He shrugged, that familiar lift of one shoulder that was both eloquent and efficient. And ridiculously attractive. "That was the easy part. Finding you here—" he tilted his head to indicate the gym "—was more difficult."

"It's raining too hard to go walking, and I needed to expend some energy. This punching bag seemed an ideal way to work off some aggravation."

"Did you picture my face on the bag?" he asked. The tiniest hint of a smile lurked in his eyes, and Susannah gritted her teeth. It was bad enough that he'd snuck up on her, that he'd watched her for Lord knows how long, without the amusement. To think that her mother had given up her location, that she hadn't called to deliver fair warning....

"I should have included my mother in the target range," she said darkly. "You must have made a mighty fine offer on The Palisades to win her over."

The smile disappeared and his expression tightened, but not only with the impact of the cynical shot. The determined set of his jawline caused her heart rate to jump about like the assaulted punching bag. "This has nothing to do with business," he said, low and even. "Your mother knows that. She's a romantic at heart."

"My mother? No. She was married to a man who cheated and lied to her for thirty years, but she never let on that she knew. She was afraid of the consequences. She liked being married to Edward Horton. She liked the position and the prestige, she put up with the negatives. My mother is a pragmatist, you see. I doubt she was ever a romantic."

"She wants you to be happy."

"And so she sent you?"

"She says you love me."

"And you belicve her?" For a long moment their eyes met and held, and for the first time, she saw the tension, the flicker of vulnerability, behind the set facade. Her pulse started to race, set alight with a new flare of hope. "Why would you take her word, Donovan, when you wouldn't believe me?"

"I was afraid to believe."

"Afraid of letting someone else close?" she guessed.

"There was that," he admitted. "And I was afraid that I could never give you anything close to the everything you talked about having with Carlisle." Serious eyes settled and steadied on hers. "After talking to you yesterday, I realised the truth. I knew the night I dropped you at your hotel. I watched you walk away and—"

His voice broke off as if he couldn't find the necessary words to describe how he'd felt, but words were unnecessary. Susannah saw all she needed in his face, in his eyes, in the fact that, finally, he was revealing himself to her.

"I didn't want you to leave," he continued, "but I didn't know what to say to make you stay."

"It would have taken only a few words."

"You say that as if it's easy." One corner of his mouth lifted ruefully, but his eyes remained intensely serious. "I've never said those words."

"Not even to Mac?"

Anguish flitted across his face and her heart rolled over. "I can't lose you, too."

Heart brimming with desperate optimism, she watched him take her hand in his, and for the first time, she saw a muscle jump in his jaw. He was nervous. Afraid. Patently terrified. A part of her ached to ease his misery, while another cautioned her to hold back and wait for everything she'd yearned to hear from this man's beautiful mouth.

"Someone suggested recently that you deserve better than me. Same person also said Charlotte Island was meant to be mine. I happen to believe that you're meant to be mine, as well." His eyes on hers quickened with a sincerity that stole her breath. "I'm not Carlisle—I don't have the ready-made family. I don't even have a home, but that's what I want with you. I don't care where we live. I can work from anywhere. I'm adaptable."

"You're independent," she cautioned. "You told me the weekend we met that you don't need a home."

"Back then I probably believed it, but that was before Mac revealed herself, before I was forced to slow down and take stock of what mattered. Before you made me reconsider the meaning of *everything*." His clasp on her fingers tightened. The expression in his eyes held her transfixed, wanting, hoping, wishing. "When I came back to Stranger's Bay, my only thought was finding a way to get The Palisades. Then I met you. I wanted you. I made excuses. I told myself it was only about ending the wedding so I could get the contract. But I couldn't stand the thought of you with another man."

Susannah's heart dipped. "You couldn't stand losing out."

"You stood up for yourself, for your principles, and that only made me love you more."

"Wanting me isn't love, Donovan."

"I love you," he said again, this time slowly and clearly, with conviction strong in his eyes. "You told me on the phone yesterday that you need to improve your core strength, but your strength is one of the things I love in you."

She started to shake her head, but he stayed her with a look.

"You're strong when it matters. You left your father's business when you no longer respected him. You didn't take the easy path, accepting his money. You walked away from a perfect marriage arrangement because you love me."

Reading the question in his eyes, she touched a hand to his face. "I do, but—"

"No buts," he said softly. "You deserve a man who loves you with everything he is, who wants to make a home and a family with you." And there, with the soldierly rows of treadmills and StairMasters and weight stations for witnesses, he went down on one knee. "I love you, Susannah, and I'm asking you to be my wife."

"Are there any clauses attached?" she asked solemnly, despite the wild racing of her heart.

"There is one about wearing my ring." Like a conjurer, he dipped into his pocket and produced a perfect white solitaire. "On your finger, a sign of commitment."

He slid the ring onto her finger, and she lifted a tremulous hand so the diamond caught the light and dazzled through her sudden tears. "It's perfect."

"It's forever," he said.

"Yes," she managed around the tearful jubilation that threatened to overwhelm her. "I know that."

"Is that a yes, you will marry me? Yes, you will be my wife?"

"Yes. Yes. I love you, Donovan. I have always loved you."

Finally, as those words took hold, the tension around his eyes eased into a smile. "I love you, too, Susannah. That's the answer, isn't it?"

"To every question."

Slowly he came to his feet and engulfed her in an embrace for a long moment before lifting her into his arms. "Where are you taking me?" she asked on a shriek when he swung her around in a wide arc. The smile on his face and in her heart turned her giddier still.

"To your room."

"To pack?" she asked, and her arms were around his neck, her face nuzzled close to his.

"Eventually."

"Hmm," she mused. "Are you thinking of an exercise I might enjoy more than the gym?"

He laughed, a wicked, smoky chuckle mirrored in his eyes as they looked down into hers. "I'm thinking that now I have you right where I want you. And I am never letting you go."

* * * * *

Don't miss Bronwyn's next miniseries,
available from Desire,
March 2009

Look for LAST WOLF WATCHING
by Rhyannon Byrd—the exciting conclusion in the
BLOODRUNNERS *miniseries*
from Silhouette Nocturne.

Follow Michaela and Brody on their fierce journey to
find the truth and face the demons from the past,
as they reach the heart of the battle between the
Runners and the rogues.

Here is a sneak preview of book three,
LAST WOLF WATCHING.

Michaela squinted, struggling to see through the impenetrable darkness. Everyone looked toward the Elders, but she knew Brody Carter still watched her. Michaela could feel the power of his gaze. Its heat. Its strength. And something that felt strangely like anger, though he had no reason to have any emotion toward her. Strangers from different worlds, brought together beneath the heavy silver moon on a night made for hell itself. That was their only connection.

The second she finished that thought, she knew it was a lie. But she couldn't deal with it now. Not tonight. Not when her whole world balanced on the edge of destruction.

Willing her backbone to keep her upright, Michaela Doucet focussed on the towering blaze of a roaring bonfire that rose from the far side of the clearing, its orange flames burning with maniacal zeal against the inky black curtain of the night. Many of the Lycans had already shifted into their preternatural shapes, their fur-covered bodies standing like monstrous shadows at the edges of the forest as they waited with restless expectancy for her brother.

Her nineteen-year-old brother, Max, had been attacked by a rogue werewolf—a Lycan who preyed upon humans for food. Max had been bitten in the attack, which meant he was no longer human, but a breed of creature that existed between the two worlds of man and beast, much like the Bloodrunners themselves.

The Elders parted, and two hulking shapes emerged from the trees. In their wolf forms, the Lycans stood over seven feet tall, their legs bent at an odd angle as they stalked forward. They each held a thick chain that had been wound around their inside wrists, the twin lengths leading back into the shadows. The Lycans had taken no more than a few steps when they jerked on the chains, and her brother appeared.

Bound like an animal.

Biting at her trembling lower lip, she glanced left, then right, surprised to see that others had joined her. Now the Bloodrunners and their family and friends stood as a united force against the Silvercrest pack, which had yet to accept the fact that something sinister was eating away at its foundation—something that would rip down the protective walls that separated their world from the humans'. It occurred to Michaela that loyalties were being announced tonight—a separation made between those who would stand with the Runners in their fight against the rogues and those who blindly supported the pack's refusal to face reality. But all she could focus on was her brother. Max looked so hurt...so terrified.

"Leave him alone," she screamed, her soft-soled, black satin slip-ons struggling for purchase in the damp earth as she rushed toward Max, only to find herself lifted off the ground when a hard, heavily muscled arm clamped around her waist from behind, pulling her clear off her feet. "Damn it, let me down!" she snarled, unable to take her eyes off her brother as the golden-eyed Lycan kicked him.

Mindless with heartache and rage, Michaela clawed at the arm holding her, kicking her heels against whatever part of her captor's legs she could reach. "Stop it," a deep, husky voice grunted in her ear. "You're not helping him by losing it. I give you my word he'll survive the ceremony, but you have to keep it together."

"Nooooo!" she screamed, too hysterical to listen to reason. "You're monsters! All of you! Look what you've done to him! How dare you! *How dare you!*"

The arm tightened with a powerful flex of muscle, cinching her waist. Her breath sucked in on a sharp, wailing gasp.

"Shut up before you get both yourself and your brother killed. I will *not* let that happen. Do you understand me?" her captor growled, shaking her so hard that her teeth clicked together. "Do you understand me, Doucet?"

"Damn it," she cried, stricken as she watched one of the guards grab Max by his hair. Around them Lycans huffed and growled as they watched the spectacle, while others outright howled for the show to begin.

"That's enough!" the voice seethed in her ear. "They'll tear you apart before you even reach him, and I'll be damned if I'm going to stand here and watch you die."

Suddenly, through the haze of fear and agony and outrage in her mind, she finally recognized who'd caught her. *Brody.*

He held her in his arms, her body locked against his powerful form, her back to the burning heat of his chest. A low, keening sound of anguish tore through her, and her head dropped forward as hoarse sobs of pain ripped from her throat. "Let me go. I have to help him. *Please*," she begged brokenly, knowing only that she needed to get to Max. "Let me go, Brody."

He muttered something against her hair, his breath warm against her scalp, and Michaela could have sworn it was a single word… But she must have heard wrong. She was too upset. Too furious. Too terrified. She must be out of her mind.

Because it sounded as if he'd quietly snarled the word *never.*

HARLEQUIN® Romance®

Western Weddings

Jason Welborn was convinced that his business partner's daughter, Jenny, had come to claim her share in the business. But Jenny seemed determined to win him over, and the more he tried to push her away, the more feisty Jenny's response. Slowly but surely she was starting to get under Jason's skin....

Look for

Coming Home to the Cattleman

by

JUDY CHRISTENBERRY

Available May wherever you buy books.

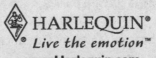

HARLEQUIN®
Live the emotion™
www.eHarlequin.com

HRI7511

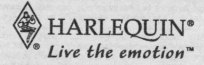

REQUEST YOUR FREE BOOKS!

2 FREE NOVELS PLUS 2 FREE GIFTS!

Passionate, Powerful, Provocative!

YES! Please send me 2 FREE Silhouette Desire® novels and my 2 FREE gifts (gifts are worth about $10). After receiving them, if I don't wish to receive any more books, I can return the shipping statement marked "cancel". If I don't cancel, I will receive 6 brand-new novels every month and be billed just $4.05 per book in the U.S. or $4.74 per book in Canada, plus 25¢ shipping and handling per book and applicable taxes, if any*. That's a savings of almost 15% off the cover price! I understand that accepting the 2 free books and gifts places me under no obligation to buy anything. I can always return a shipment and cancel at any time. Even if I never buy another book, the two free books and gifts are mine to keep forever.

225 SDN ERVX 326 SDN ERVM

Name	(PLEASE PRINT)	
Address		Apt. #
City	State/Prov.	Zip/Postal Code

Signature (if under 18, a parent or guardian must sign)

Mail to the Silhouette Reader Service:

IN U.S.A.: P.O. Box 1867, Buffalo, NY 14240-1867
IN CANADA: P.O. Box 609, Fort Erie, Ontario L2A 5X3

Not valid to current subscribers of Silhouette Desire books.

Want to try two free books from another line?
Call 1-800-873-8635 or visit www.morefreebooks.com.

* Terms and prices subject to change without notice. N.Y. residents add applicable sales tax. Canadian residents will be charged applicable provincial taxes and GST. This offer is limited to one order per household. All orders subject to approval. Credit or debit balances in a customer's account(s) may be offset by any other outstanding balance owed by or to the customer. Please allow 4 to 6 weeks for delivery. Offer available while quantities last.

Your Privacy: Silhouette Books is committed to protecting your privacy. Our Privacy Policy is available online at www.eHarlequin.com or upon request from the Reader Service. From time to time we make our lists of customers available to reputable third parties who may have a product or service of interest to you. If you would prefer we not share your name and address, please check here. ☐

SDES08

![Silhouette]

SPECIAL EDITION™

♥✚ THE WILDER FAMILY
Healing Hearts in Walnut River

Social worker Isobel Suarez was proud to work at Walnut River General Hospital, so when Neil Kane showed up from the attorney general's office to investigate insurance fraud, she was up in arms. Until she melted in his arms, and things got very tricky...

Look for

HER MR. RIGHT?

by

KAREN ROSE SMITH

Available May wherever books are sold.

Inside ROMANCE

Stay up-to-date on all your
romance reading news!

Inside Romance is a FREE quarterly newsletter
highlighting our upcoming series releases
and promotions.

Visit
www.eHarlequin.com/InsideRomance
to sign up to receive our complimentary newsletter today!

IRNI 107